cupcake
cousins

cupcake cousins

by Kate Hannigan

illustrated by
Brooke Boynton Hughes

SCHOLASTIC INC.

ISBN 978-0-545-92549-5

Text copyright © 2014 by Kate Hannigan.
Illustrations copyright © 2014 by Brooke Boynton Hughes. All rights reserved.
Published by Scholastic Inc., 557 Broadway, New York, NY 10012, by arrangement with
Hyperion Books for Children, an imprint of Disney Book Group. SCHOLASTIC and
associated logos are trademarks and/or registered trademarks of Scholastic Inc.

12 11 10 9 8 7 6 5 4 3 2 1   15 16 17 18 19 20/0

Printed in the U.S.A.   40

First Scholastic printing, October 2015

for cousins olivia & chloe,
and michigan summers
—k.h.

for mom, dad, christopher, and bill
and for the baukol cousins, who love a good wedding
—b.b.h.

Contents

1. In the Pink 1

2. Let the Vacationing Begin! 17

3. A Not-So-Sweet Start 30

4. When the Fireflies Come Out 40

5. The Eyes Have It 49

6. Blueberry Surprise 63

7. Things Don't Always Go Smoothie 79

8. Roasting Marshmallows 86

9. A Run-Through 99

10. Good Morning, Sunshine 113

11. Just Peachy 126

12. A Periwinkle Party 138

13. Hummingbirds and Hungry Bears 148

14. Helping Hands, Paws, and Jaws 156

15. Boogie Boards, Sand Castles, and Summer Secrets 170

16. Mr. Henry's Shed 181

17. Making Peace 184

18. Wedding Day, Very, Very Early 198

19. Off to the Hospital 213

20. Knock Knock. Who's There? 217

21. Showtime! 233

22. The Flour Girls 237

23. A Few More Summer Surprises 257

cupcake
cousins

The Bumpus family
invites you to join in
the celebration of the marriage
of their daughter

Rose Bumpus
to Jonathan Baxter

at 11am in the morning
on Saturday, August the 23rd
at the Whispering Pines Bed & Breakfast
in Saugatuck, Michigan

the wedding party

flower girls	Willow Sweeney, *niece of the bride*
	Delia Dees, *niece of the bride*
junior bridesmaids	Violet Sweeney, *niece of the bride*
	Darlene Dees, *niece of the bride*
ring bearer	Sweet William Sweeney, *nephew of the bride*
matrons of honor	Agapanthus Bumpus Sweeney, *sister of the bride*
	Gardenia Bumpus Dees, *sister of the bride*
groomsmen	Liam Sweeney, *brother-in-law of the bride*
	Delvan Dees, *brother-in-law of the bride*
best men	Peter Baxter, *brother of the groom*
	Kevin Baxter, *brother of the groom*

Chapter 1
in the pink

Willow scowled at the flower-girl dress like it was growing in a patch of poison ivy. Every time she looked at it, she had the same thoughts.

That it was pink.

That it was awful.

That it should not come anywhere close to her skin.

"You must be so excited for Aunt Rosie's wedding," her mom said as she stuffed more clothes into an already overflowing suitcase.

Willow was sitting on her parents' bed in a silent standoff with the pink gown. Sandwiched between pieces of oversized luggage, she glared at the wedding outfit draped over the chair across from her.

Her bubble gum–bright dress glared right back.

"This year's vacation is going to be so special," her mom continued, giving Willow's head a quick pat as she transferred swimming trunks from one suitcase to the other. "I can just feel it in my bones. Extra special."

Willow loved her aunt Rosie. And she loved their summer vacations to Michigan. But the thought of having to be a flower girl and wear that awful pink gown made her skin break out in blotchy hives.

"And Delia will look so adorable in her dress, too," her mother added with a pause that Willow considered a bit dramatic. "Just thinking of you girls leading the way down the aisle together . . ." Her voice trailed off.

Willow imagined her cousin Delia in the same poufy dress. At least Delia, with her black hair and dark brown skin, could wear the color. But pink clothes on freckle-faced, copper-haired Willow just

made her look sunburned. And even if they could dye those frilly gowns green, nothing would change how babyish they were.

"Preschoolers would look better in these baby dresses than two fourth graders," Delia had grumbled when they talked on the phone.

Fourth-grade flower girls?

It was too much for Willow to bear.

Maybe Aunt Rosie thought the gowns came packaged with the cute little toddlers in the catalog pictures. Since Willow's family lived in Chicago and Delia's was in Detroit, Aunt Rosie had done the dress shopping on her own— picking the flower-girl gowns from a magazine without seeing how they looked on the actual flower girls themselves.

"I'll go finish my packing," Willow announced, suddenly eager to get away from the dress. She dashed down the hall and over the body of Bernice, their 117-pound Bernese mountain dog, who was delicately chewing the shoelaces of a blue sneaker like she was

eating spaghetti. "You can help me, Bernice," she whispered.

Willow pushed a pile of clothes off her bed and into her open suitcase, making room for Bernice and the sneaker. Plopping onto a pillow beside them, she knocked the suitcase shut with a "Humph." Why couldn't she and Delia be junior bridesmaids and wear purple dresses like Violet and Darlene? Their sisters were only a few years older, but they were being treated like big shots, while Willow and Delia were stuck with frilly princess gowns, neon-pink shoes that could be seen from outer space, and flowery baskets for tossing rose petals.

"And Willow," her mom called down the hall, "bring me your pink ballet flats and that sweet little rosebud basket. They're the last things on my checklist for the wedding."

Willow's mom was a school librarian, which meant she thrived on order. And it meant she was never without a checklist.

"I don't mean to rub it in," chuckled Violet, who was standing in Willow's doorway now and clearly rubbing it in, "but your dress is pink like a dog's tongue. No offense to Bernice."

Bernice raised a furry black ear in Willow's direction, as if she couldn't believe the things Violet said these days either. Then, letting the slobbery sneaker drop, Bernice licked Willow's knee, and they both stared across at Violet until she got the hint to leave.

"Well, I'm out of here," Violet announced, snapping her gum and heading down the hallway to deposit her gown with their mom. "Hurry up and finish packing, by the way. Dad is already loading the car."

Willow tried not to focus on the bubble gum Violet was chewing. But it was hard to miss— blindingly pink, just like the flower-girl dresses. She and Delia had been fighting the gowns since July, when they had arrived in the mail.

"No way. Never. *Uh-uh*," they had repeated.

They'd already considered putting the dresses in the washing machine to shrink them so they wouldn't fit. Or leaving them outside to bake in the hot sun so the color might fade. They'd even plotted sending them to zoo camp with Delia and letting the penguins use them for nests.

But their moms had told them the same thing every time—that this was Aunt Rosie's wedding, so Aunt Rosie was the boss. "When you get married, girls, then you get to make all the decisions."

Get married? That thought made Willow itchy all over again.

"I'm still waiting, Willow," her mom called again from the suitcases. "I want to check those things off my list."

Willow wished she could feed that checklist to Bernice.

Flopping onto her stomach and sliding underneath the bed, all the way to the back corner, Willow dug out the neon-pink wedding shoes. "I'll surrender these," she told Bernice, "but I draw the line at the goofy basket."

Willow tossed the wedding shoes onto her mom's bed next to Violet's purple gown and bounced her suitcase down the stairs. Then she gathered up the last of her vacation essentials—her tattered notebook full of recipes, her favorite blue sun hat, and a lucky penny—and tucked them into her polka-dotted messenger bag. Throwing the strap over her shoulder, she headed with Bernice for the car.

"Now give it back," Violet was saying as Willow

climbed into the backseat between her sister and their little brother, Sweet William. "I said you could wear my medal for a minute, and that's what I meant. Sixty seconds!"

"You count too fast," Sweet William complained. But he finally relented and passed the red-white-and-blue ribbon back to Violet. A gold medal the size of a pancake dangled in front of Willow's face for a few moments as it transferred from her brother's pudgy hand to her sister's long and graceful one.

"Why are you bringing your swimming medals to the beach house?" Willow asked, trying to hide her annoyance. She had been looking forward to a vacation from her sister's latest triumphs.

"Mom wants me to show Grandma, Grandpa, and everybody what I've won this summer," Violet said. Then she added, "I'm only bringing a few, since it would take practically a whole suitcase to carry all of them."

Willow reached into her bag and pulled out the lucky penny. It suddenly looked very small.

"What ya got there, Willow?" asked Sweet William, wriggling into his booster seat and hooking the straps.

"It's called a wheat penny," she said. "I picked it up off the sidewalk by the dojo just before karate class yesterday. I think it's extra lucky."

"A sweet penny?" gushed her brother, who was always mixing up his words. "It's named for me! Can I have it?"

"*Wheat*, not sweet," Violet said irritably. "You've got to listen better, Sweet William."

Willow patiently ran her finger over the

etching on the face of the copper coin to help him understand. "This penny has stalks of wheat on it. It's really rare. So I think that makes it really lucky, too."

The back hatch to the station wagon was open, and their parents were hovering behind them, arranging the suitcases and the plastic bags that held all the wedding outfits. Willow rubbed the lucky wheat penny with her thumb and made a wish that Bernice would gnaw an enormous hole in her flower-girl gown during the two-hour drive to Michigan.

"Pennies are basically worthless," declared Violet, who as a sixth-grader was starting middle school and therefore always setting Willow straight. "And would you please strap in? We can't head for Saugatuck until you've clicked."

Saugatuck. Willow looked out the window as the car pulled away from the curb and imagined they were already there, beneath the thick canopy of trees and gazing back across Lake Michigan toward Chicago. She loved everything about the place, even how the name sounded on her tongue.

SAW-gah-tuck.

The word itself was summertime: cousins and grandparents, aunts and uncles, everybody sleeping all together in the old white house called Whispering Pines. They'd been renting there for so many summers that even the owner, Henry Rickles, was like family.

In her mind, Willow made her own checklist of how she would spend the week with Delia. Picking peaches at the orchards, boogie-boarding in the lake, catching fireflies in the moonlight. And just like last summer, they'd make pancakes every morning and desserts every night. Side by side with Delia in the Whispering Pines kitchen—that was probably her favorite place to be. Though baking cakes with her dad in Chicago, whisks in hand, ran a close second.

Or maybe it was the other way around. Willow couldn't decide.

"Great whoopee pies yesterday, Willow," her dad said, grinning and readjusting the rearview mirror so he could see her in the backseat. "That buttermilk trick worked, didn't it?"

"It was amazing," Willow agreed. "How did you know that mixing lemon juice and milk would be a good thing?"

Willow's mom said she had never heard of using sour milk in place of buttermilk in a recipe. "But then again, your dad would know. He's the family chef around here."

"Willow, too," he said with a wink. "We both are. She knows about as much as I do by now."

Willow grinned, turning that thought around in her head. *Chef Willow Sweeney.* She winked back at her dad in the mirror, careful not to whisper the words out loud. If she did, she'd never hear the end of it from Violet.

"I hope she knows not to add peppermint extract to the scrambled eggs anymore," Violet announced, shuddering at the memory. "That was a hard lesson—for all of us."

Willow gazed out the window at the passing

billboards. "You never know how something will turn out until you give it a try," she said softly.

"Well, try again on that yellow cake you baked last week. Did anyone taste that thing?" Violet made a gagging sound and dropped her head to the side like she was dying. "Dreadful!"

Willow did her best to ignore her older sister. Again. But lately Violet and her comments were getting harder to brush off. Willow sank lower in her seat, fighting the urge to climb into the very back and ride all the way to Saugatuck with Bernice.

Willow Sweeney's Practically Perfect Whoopee Pies

Ingredients:

2 cups all-purpose flour

½ cup unsweetened cocoa powder

2 teaspoons baking powder

½ teaspoon salt

12 tablespoons (1½ sticks) unsalted butter, softened but not melted

1 cup sugar

1 egg

1 teaspoon vanilla extract

½ cup buttermilk or sour milk*

For the filling:

8 ounces (1 brick) cream cheese

8 tablespoons (1 stick) unsalted butter, softened but not melted

1 teaspoon vanilla

2 cups powdered sugar

* To make the sour milk, pour 1 tablespoon lemon juice in a measuring cup, then add enough nonfat or low-fat milk to equal 1 cup liquid.

Directions:

1. Make sure you have an adult's help.

2. Heat the oven to 400 degrees. Mix the flour, cocoa powder, baking powder, and salt in one bowl.

3. Using an electric mixer in a second bowl, beat together the butter and sugar until light and fluffy. Slowly pour in the dry ingredients from the first bowl. Add the egg, vanilla, and buttermilk or sour milk. Beat until it's all combined.

4. Drop the batter, about 2 tablespoons at a time, onto two baking sheets lined with parchment paper. Make about 24 cookie-size cakes. Smooth and flatten slightly. Bake about 10 minutes. Cool about 10 minutes.

5. Filling: With an electric mixer, beat the cream cheese, softened butter, and vanilla, slowly adding the powdered sugar. Beat on high until smooth and creamy. Add more sugar to taste.

6. While the cookies are cooling, refrigerate the filling for about a half hour.

7. Gently spread the filling across a cooled cookie-cake. Then put another cookie-cake on top, sandwiching the filling. Repeat until there aren't any cakes left.

Makes a dozen whoopee pies.

Chapter 2
let the vacationing begin!

a short while later came the shout Willow was waiting for. "Look sharp, everybody!" her dad called. "This is the turnoff for Whispering Pines!"

By the time the car reached the final curve, Willow was too excited for their vacation to stay annoyed. She squeezed Sweet William's knee in anticipation and rolled down his window to breathe in the August air.

"Don't crush my crickets," he giggled, pushing her hand away from the pocket of his shorts. "They're on vacation, too."

Willow's dad honked the horn as the car bounced

its way down the long, tree-lined drive. A dusty smell wafted in from the gravel crunching underneath the wheels. Willow scooted up in her seat, leaning between her parents' headrests to get a good look at the three-story house as it appeared through the thick pine trees.

She loved this moment, the way the pebbly driveway stretched out before them like a promise. It was always these seconds—just when the tall white Victorian came into view, the blue water of Lake Michigan fanning out behind it—that Willow replayed again and again in her head like a movie throughout the long school year.

She squeezed her penny and made a wish that they could stay forever.

"Aggie's here," came Grandma's shout from the porch. And Willow saw her grandmother waving at the car, both hands covered in bright green gardening gloves.

Violet flung her door open, and the girls were clambering out of the car before their dad had even turned off the engine. Their mom was already out of her seat belt too, dashing across the yard toward her two squealing sisters, Aunt Rosie and Aunt Deenie. Only Grandpa called the three of them by their real names, Agapanthus, Rose, and Gardenia. "By any other name," he liked to say, "my three flowers wouldn't smell half as sweet."

Thwack!

Willow smiled at the familiar smack of the screen door off the side of the house. It sounded like a cap gun announcing the start of a race. The best part of summer vacation was finally beginning.

Sweet William began pushing his way through the crowd of relatives toward Grandpa and Grandma, whose straw hats made them easy to find. Grandma's wide, floppy brim was ringed with sunflowers.

Bernice followed closely at Sweet William's heels, and Willow could hear her brother issuing noisy complaints about too many knees blocking his route. Willow felt herself pulled into the friendly chaos too, weaving her way through dozens of family members who were busy kissing cheeks and patting backs. Some of the faces were unfamiliar.

"Sweet William," Grandma said with a hug, "I'd like you to meet some of the groom's family."

Willow slipped past them, deciding to circle back later for her own introduction. Because just then, there was one person she wanted to find more than anyone else in the world.

Where was Delia?

She heard the shout first. *"Willooooow!"*

Then she saw a flash of black braids and brown arms just before she felt the impact.

"Delia!" Willow coughed. "I'm so happy—" And that's all she could get out as both girls tumbled onto the lawn, choking with laughter and flopping about like a couple of rainbow trout. Bernice raced over and began to bark and circle the two of them, licking Delia's face whenever she saw an opening.

"See what I have to live with?" complained Violet,

who had already paired off with Delia's seventh-grade sister, Darlene. "It's like we have two five-year-olds in the family instead of just one."

Sweet William stepped over, seeming unsure whether to be insulted or not.

"There is a reason," said Darlene, sliding her sunglasses down her nose, "why you are flower girls and we are junior bridesmaids."

Willow got to her feet, then reached a hand out to help Delia up. They draped their arms around each other's shoulders and wandered toward the house, Delia tugging clumps of green clover from Willow's curls.

"Darlene is about as fun as a mosquito bite," she said. "Don't listen to her."

"Violet is the same," Willow agreed, glancing back at their sisters. "Like she's so mature and I'm a little pest or something."

"They won't treat us like babies after this week," Delia said. "Once we get out of the flower-girl jobs and do something better, Darlene and Violet will be so jealous."

"And we have good luck to make it happen." Willow smiled, pulling the wheat penny from her pocket. "It's even more powerful than a regular lucky penny."

Delia was just giving the wheat penny a kiss when Aunt Rosie appeared.

"How are my darling flower girls?" she squealed. "I am so excited to see you in those pink dresses. Don't you just love them?"

Delia elbowed Willow.

Willow elbowed back.

Delia tugged on her two braids, then began chewing on the tip of one of them. Willow was left to fill the awkward silence.

She wasn't sure where to start. For the past month, she and Delia had been searching for ways to get out of the flower-girl jobs. They had tried to take Sweet William's role as ring bearer, but he'd hidden the fancy pillow and wouldn't tell them where it was. They'd even taught themselves how to play a mushy wedding song with Willow on the violin and Delia on the flute. But that hadn't sounded so good.

Finally, Willow and Delia had decided that if Aunt Rosie knew how amazing they were in the kitchen, she would beg them to trade those ugly pink gowns for white aprons. "She just needs to taste our food. Just one little lemon tart," the cousins had conspired. "Then she'll realize that all our talents are being wasted."

But here was Aunt Rosie, standing right in front

of them, waiting for an answer. And Willow was speechless.

"The dresses really are . . . something," Willow began.

She wanted to be honest. But Willow knew she couldn't say how truly ugly they were without hurting Aunt Rosie's feelings. First there was the little flap of material at the neck that her mom called a Peter Pan collar. (Willow never understood why Peter didn't want to grow up.) Then there were the big pink roses sewn around the waist. Not to mention those long, silky ribbons—Willow and Delia were going to look like kites instead of kids!

Willow saw her aunt's eager expression and tried again.

"You know, Aunt Rosie, Delia and I are nearly ten now . . . Delia is already nine and ten-twelfths, which is really five-sixths . . ."

Aunt Rosie tilted her head to the side, looking a little puzzled.

"Go on," she said.

Willow felt stuck.

"We're much too . . ."

How could she tell Aunt Rosie they weren't little kids anymore? How could she explain that flower-girl duties were for kindergartners—for five-year-olds like Sweet William? Not for girls who were practically in middle school and just about ready to start driving a car.

"We want to talk to you about the wedding," Delia finally said, plucking the braid from her mouth and using her clear, calm crossing-guard voice. Not only was Delia good at walking kids safely through traffic, she was great at getting a grown-up's undivided attention. "Willow and I would rather make a—"

"Cupcake, where have you been? Stolen away by the flower girls, I see."

Aunt Rosie's fiancé, Jonathan Baxter, suddenly appeared, beaming at Delia and Willow with his dimpled smile. Jonathan had won them both over last Thanksgiving, after he'd taught them how to juggle dinner rolls. And he had been the only one at the table to ask for a second helping of their pumpkin-cheesecake tarts, graciously overlooking how they'd left out the cream cheese.

"Great to see you, Uncle Jonathan," Willow said with a bouncy grin.

"Not uncle yet," Delia corrected. "Technically, there are still five more days."

"Four days, twenty-two hours, and thirty-one minutes," Jonathan said with a shy smile. Willow

noticed his grin was slightly crooked, and she decided that was another quality she liked about Jonathan. "Now if you'll excuse us, ladies, it looks as if our beautiful bride-to-be is wanted on the porch for a toast."

Before they stepped away, Jonathan added, "I hope you two brought your cookbooks. I'm hungry for more tarts!"

Aunt Rosie gave them each a peck on the cheek.

"Do you still play in the kitchen, girls?" she asked. "You both have so many activities and interests. It's just adorable!"

And then Aunt Rosie and Jonathan were gone, their heads bobbing in the waves of relatives flowing onto the porch and around to the back of the house, where they had clear views of Lake Michigan.

"*Play?*" Delia asked, her eyes staring after them.

"*Adorable?*" Willow echoed. "She thinks we're still five years old, doesn't she?"

"Everybody thinks we're still five years old."

They stood in silence in the blue shadow of the

old oak tree, waiting and watching until the last relative (or was that a family friend? Willow wasn't sure) had climbed the porch steps and disappeared around the house.

"So much for talking about cupcakes," Delia said, her shoulders sagging. "Or cookies. Or cheesecakes. She has no idea what we could do for her wedding."

"Don't worry," Willow said, dashing over to their parked car and pulling her polka-dotted bag from the backseat. "There's still plenty of time to show Aunt Rosie how amazing we are."

Not only had Willow come to Whispering Pines armed with her notebook full of dessert ideas, but she had packed Aunt Rosie's favorite snack foods, too. She lifted the flap and showed Delia the Mentos, Good & Plenty candies, and fancy marshmallows tucked inside.

"We're going straight for her stomach!" Delia cheered, throwing her arm around Willow's shoulder again. "We'll start with all her favorites."

Willow threw her arm around her cousin's shoulder too, and they marched across the wide yard toward the kitchen. "And then when she gets a taste of what we can make in there, she's going to be shocked. I bet we'll save her wedding day!"

Chapter 3
a not-so-sweet start

The space was just as they remembered it from Augusts before: white marble countertops, tall white cabinets with shiny silver handles, an island in the center of it all, and above it a rack hanging from the ceiling with black and silver and copper pots dangling down like Christmas ornaments.

"Our kitchen," Delia sighed, picking up a white tea towel and folding it neatly into a tight rectangle.

"Just waiting for us," Willow agreed, running her fingers over the cold marble and accidentally sending a rolling pin spinning across the counter. Delia caught it just before it hit the floor.

Suddenly the heavy wooden door from the dining room swung open. Mr. Henry, the owner of Whispering Pines, stepped in, chatting with someone Willow didn't recognize. When he saw the girls standing there, Mr. Henry's cheeks flushed just a hint pinker than they usually were. He cleared his throat.

"Delia Dees, Willow Sweeney," he began, "I'd like to introduce you to Ms. Catherine Sutherland. Cat here is Whispering Pines's first-ever chef. She comes to us from Tupelo, Mississippi, where she ran a thriving restaurant and catering business. Now, lucky us, we have the pleasure of experiencing her food here."

Like ice cream hitting a sensitive tooth, Mr. Henry's words gave them both a jolt. Cat was a caterer? And now Whispering Pines had a full-time chef, as in a chef who ran the kitchen?

This kitchen?

Their kitchen?

"Delia and Willow have been the cooks around here in previous summers," said Mr. Henry, smiling.

"They helped me flip many a pancake in their day, and the ceiling can attest to it."

Both girls automatically looked up, as if one of the pancakes they'd flipped last August were still stuck there and ready to drop onto their heads.

"Isn't that precious," Cat said, her drawl so thick it sounded more like *pray-shuss*. "Y'all are real chefs in the making."

Cat's words were sweet as sugar, but Willow thought her face looked more like she'd tasted something sour.

"Why don't you ladies help us with the lemonade?" Mr. Henry asked. "We'll bring these out to the guests, if you girls don't mind handling the two pitchers."

Mr. Henry and Cat cautiously picked up two trays loaded down with ice-filled glasses. They carried them outside as Delia and Willow examined the lemonade.

Bits of lemon pulp had settled on the bottom, and perfectly sliced lemon rounds floated at the top. It looked fresh-squeezed, not like some powdered mix.

"But does it taste any good?" asked Delia, pouring herself a small cup.

"Aunt Rosie likes hers super sweet," Willow reminded her.

Delia took a sip. "It's decent," she admitted, smacking her lips. "But it could use more sugar."

"I knew it," Willow said with a little bounce. "Nobody has a sweet tooth like Aunt Rosie. We've got to fix it."

Willow stepped over to the row of white canisters that lined the back counter and pulled off each lid, searching for the sugar. But just as she was about to pour a mound of the white stuff into the pitchers, Delia stopped her.

"What are you thinking?" Delia gasped. "You can't just go throwing things in. We're chefs, Willow. Chefs measure!"

Willow rolled her eyes, wanting to remind her cousin that chefs experiment, too. "Fine, but hurry up and find a measuring cup. We've got to fix this before Cat comes back! We can't let her get in our way with Aunt Rosie." And jabbing a long wooden spoon in the air, she added, "We've got to show everybody who has the real talent in this kitchen."

Delia opened drawers until she found a shiny silver measuring cup. Then she measured two precise scoops of white crystals from the canister Willow held, dumping each one into the first pitcher. She scooped two more, eyeing them and dumping them into the second one.

After Willow gave each pitcher a quick stir, the cousins stepped out onto the porch and around to the back of the house. Grandpa and Grandma were in their usual white wicker chairs near the big back door, so Willow filled their glasses first. Delia carried her jug over to Aunt Rosie, who was sitting with Jonathan and Sweet William. Bernice sprawled at their feet.

Mr. Henry stood near Grandpa and talked glowingly about Cat and the restaurant she'd run down in Mississippi before she moved to Saugatuck last fall. He told them about her cranberry scones and her lemon crepes, her peach pies and her mint ice cream. Delia's dad, Uncle Delvan, explained to Cat that his family was from Mississippi too, and how his grandfather had moved the family north to Michigan back in the 1920s.

"Came to Detroit to work in the car industry. Part of what they now call the Black Migration," said Uncle Delvan. "I'm a third-generation General Motors man. . . . At least, I was until the layoffs."

Once Willow and Delia had made their way to all the members of the Bumpus and Baxter families, Grandpa stood up and raised his glass.

"What do you call the flowers growing on our faces?" he began, never without a flower joke. "Tulips! So put your two lips together and make some noise for the happy couple!"

The whole porch erupted in whistles and cheers, and Jonathan gave Aunt Rosie a bashful kiss.

"First, a toast to our one and only Rose Bumpus and the man who's finally won her heart, Jonathan

Baxter. But second, let us raise a glass to Cat Sutherland and the sweet surprises that will come from the kitchen this week!"

And before Willow and Delia even got their glasses to their lips, the first surprise hit.

It was a very particular sound. And the moment Willow heard it, she knew what it was: Sweet William spraying lemonade from his mouth like he was putting out a fire.

"*Will-OOOOW!*" shouted Violet, making that familiar gagging sound. Darlene, who was tucked into the rocking chair beside Violet, coughed and clutched her throat.

"Do you think the girls had something to do with this?" Aunt Deenie asked Willow's mom. They were craning their necks and looking around for Delia and Willow, while holding their glasses as far away from their mouths as possible.

Willow saw her dad take a timid taste of the lemonade, his face crinkling up like a dried plum.

"Yes," he said, choking, "it's very possible they did."

Delia looked over at Willow and raised a single eyebrow in worry. Willow shrugged. What was going on? They silently slipped around the corner and back into the kitchen again.

Scrambling over to the far counter, Willow sized up the three white canisters. They looked identical, except that the middle one's lid was askew, like a sailor's cap. A dusting of white crystals marked a trail from its base to the spot where the pitchers had stood.

"I thought we measured just the right amount," Delia began.

Willow ran her finger over the crystals, then tasted them.

"The right amount for sugar, maybe," she groaned. "But Delia, we added salt!"

Suddenly Willow heard footsteps on the porch. Then Cat Sutherland's hulking figure filled the screen door. *Thwack!* She stormed into the kitchen, pointing her finger at them.

"What in the blue blazes are you two

whippersnappers up to?" she huffed, pushing her way to where they were standing. "Are you trying to make me look bad in front of Rosie and everybody?"

Willow opened her mouth to speak but discovered her voice had fled. And Delia was no better off, pointing at the canisters and shaking her head like she was a circus mime.

Finally—thankfully!—Mr. Henry appeared beside Cat and cleared his throat.

"This might be a wonderful time," he suggested, slipping his sun hat off his head and placing it right back on again, "for you young ladies to enjoy the beach."

Chapter 4
when the fireflies
come out

hours later, after the guests had scattered and the sun was setting into Lake Michigan, Delia and Willow squeezed together into one of the wooden chairs near the bluff and tucked their bare knees into their sweatshirts.

Willow never paid much attention to the sun during the day as it made its slow march across the sky. But sitting there at the edge of the yard and looking out at the wide, watery horizon, she couldn't help but notice how the sun was in a hurry to get to bed. She counted the seconds it took for the last little lip of orange to sink into the purple-blue water.

". . . twenty-three, twenty-four, twenty-five. Gone!" Willow said. "See you tomorrow, Sunny."

They had most of the backyard to themselves. Darlene and Violet were playing a game of Scrabble with Grandma and Grandpa in the dining room. Willow heard cheers erupt now and then when someone spelled a particularly impressive word. Sweet William was working at a table on the other end of the porch, softly humming "Jingle Bells." He was busy rolling out tiny animals and people from the modeling clay he'd brought from home. Bernice stretched out under his table, her tail thumping happily now and then on the wooden porch.

"I'm glad we're here," Delia said, speaking into the neck of her sweatshirt, which she'd slid up her chin like she was a turtle hiding in its shell. "Zoo camp was fun, but the rest of the summer hasn't been so great."

Willow knew Uncle Delvan had lost his job making cars in Detroit. She'd seen the news reports: lots of people were out of work. Willow's mom worried about losing her job in the school library. And Willow had heard her dad say that newspapers were disappearing. If they did, his job as a food critic for the *Chicago Tribune* would disappear with them.

"I know we'll have a great time this week, Delia. Try not to worry about things."

The breeze off the lake was cool. Delia shivered and wrapped her arms tighter around her knees. Willow slid her toes under her sweatshirt and snuggled in closer to her cousin. They sat in silence watching the water.

Their fathers' voices drifted through the open windows. A few words here and there took shape, swirling into the summer night like moths: *layoffs*, *bills*, *money*. Willow wondered what their mothers were talking about down on the beach below.

"They're fighting a lot these days," Delia said, her eyes fixed on Aunt Deenie's silhouette. "They never do anything together. Mom is working extra shifts at the hospital to pay for stuff. And Dad's sad a lot. He puts on a good face so Darlene and I don't worry. But he can't fool us. We know it's bad. Darlene even has to change schools, since we can't afford the other one."

Willow put her arm around Delia and leaned her head gently against her cousin's. They gazed up at the first stars of the night. Delia said the brightest one was Venus. And that made Willow wonder—was wishing on a planet more powerful than wishing on a star?

Without her cousin noticing, Willow reached into her shorts pocket. With the wheat penny in her hand

and the planet-star above, she made a silent wish. For Uncle Delvan and for Aunt Deenie. But mostly for Delia.

"Your dad will find work soon, I just know he will. And things will be good again, I promise."

"I sure hope so," Delia said, tucking her chin back into her sweatshirt. "It can't get much worse."

Hushed voices rode on the breeze again, only this time they weren't coming from the house behind them. They were coming from the steep staircase ahead leading up from the beach. Willow's mom and Aunt Deenie were finally returning, a little breathless from the climb.

"I don't want to give up on him, Aggie," sniffled Aunt Deenie, wiping her eyes.

Delia and Willow sat unnoticed in the darkness. A few fireflies flickered nearby, blinking secret messages back and forth as the girls' moms shuffled past.

Delia pulled her sweatshirt up, her whole head disappearing inside.

Willow worried about her relatives from Detroit. While *D* seemed to be the letter for Delia's family, Willow hoped it wouldn't stand for the worst *D* word she could think of.

Divorce.

"What's that noise?" asked Willow, yanking the sheets up to her chin.

It was nearly midnight, and she and Delia had just turned off the lights and climbed into their squeaky side-by-side beds in the room they shared upstairs. It was on the second floor, just beneath Violet and Darlene's third-floor bedroom. The three wide-open windows faced the lake, and a breeze lifted the white curtains now and then. Willow could see the stars from where she lay on her pillow.

"Listen, Delia! There it is again. What can that be? Is something wrong with the air conditioning? Or do you think a squirrel is trapped in our wall?"

Delia let out a laugh and rolled over to face Willow in the blue darkness.

"Willow, are you kidding me? That noise is Lake Michigan—that's the water lapping on the beach. This old house doesn't even have air conditioning!"

Both girls went silent, neither one moving an inch as they listened to the night noises. Now that Delia reminded her, Willow recognized the peaceful sound of lake water washing up their stretch of shoreline and back out again. There was a comforting rhythm

to the waves, and it gave Willow the feeling of rocking back and forth in a hammock.

Willow's thoughts lingered on Delia and what her family was going through. But then they wandered to her own worries.

What if they couldn't get out of the flower-girl jobs this week? What if they had to walk down the aisle wearing those awful pink dresses, with everyone smiling at them like they were a couple of kindergartners? She flopped over onto her side, punching her pillow a few times to flatten it.

What if she and Delia had made the new caterer so angry that she kept them out of the kitchen the whole week? Was Willow going to miss out on the chance to work with a real chef?

Willow turned over in the other direction now, the springs making a jangly sound beneath her. The noise reminded her of Violet's gold medals clanging together. Violet, who was good at everything. Violet, the winner. Willow squeezed her eyes tight, trying to clear her mind.

If only she could do something right like Violet. Maybe she wouldn't have to win a gold medal for it. But it would be nice to see her mom and dad proud of her, too, for once.

Chapter 5
the eyes have it

Willow and Delia opened their bedroom door the next morning and found Uncle Delvan standing there, fumbling with a package. Willow eyed the flat square, about three feet wide and wrapped in glossy white paper, and she knew right away it was a wedding present.

"Mind if I hide this in your room, girls?" he asked. "Rosie is hanging her wedding dress in our closet. She's afraid Jonathan will see it before Saturday if she leaves it in her room, and that will bring bad luck. Some people around here are so superstitious."

Willow patted the pocket that held their lucky penny, and she and Delia smiled. Aunt Rosie definitely wasn't the only superstitious one.

"Is it one of your paintings?" Willow asked, helping slide the present under Delia's bed (which somehow, Willow noticed, was already made). "I wish you would show me how to paint and draw. You'd make a great art teacher."

Uncle Delvan ran his fingers over his goatee and shrugged. "I never thought about working with kids the way your mom does, Willow. Maybe that's a job I should consider."

Just then Bernice came wagging into the room. She greeted Uncle Delvan and Delia with nudges and sniffs, then stretched out at Willow's feet.

"What's that pink thing Bernice is lying on?" Uncle Delvan asked, peering down at the jumble of fabric on the floor beneath Bernice's black, brown, and white fur.

"Oh, that?" Delia asked, trying to sound innocent. "That's just one of the . . . *umm*. . . thingies."

Uncle Delvan shook his head. "You've got to take better care of those dresses, girls," he said, calling Bernice to follow him as he left the room. "If Rosie sees that, she might get the impression you don't want to be flower girls in her wedding."

Delia gave Willow a knowing look; then she hooked the gown on a peg by the closet.

The cousins set off downstairs, following the delicious breakfast smells that drifted through the house. They had just reached the dining room when they ran into Violet and Darlene coming out of the kitchen. Willow could swear she saw their lip gloss glisten, catching the summer sun like stained-glass windows.

"You guys look fancy," she said, trying to ignore the medals Violet had draped around her neck. Willow bit her bottom lip, wishing she'd brushed her teeth instead of sharing Mentos with Delia.

"Did you take a shower already?" asked Delia in surprise. But it was obvious their big sisters had bathed. Willow could smell a hint of soap from where they were standing. It mixed strangely with the smell of bacon coming from the other side of the kitchen door.

Willow wasn't exactly sure why anyone would bother showering when they were just going to go jump in the lake later anyway. She pulled her blue sun hat from her back pocket and tugged it down over her tangle of curls, hoping to hide the fact that—as with

her teeth—a brush had not touched her hair.

"We actually believe in bathing," Darlene said sarcastically as she applied another coat of glittery gloss to her lips. "Someday you might come around to our way of thinking, Delia."

As the Dees sisters squared off—Darlene smirking, Delia sneering—Willow couldn't help but notice how similar they looked. Same long arms and legs. Same heart-shaped faces as Aunt Deenie. Same graceful way of moving. That wasn't how it was with the Sweeney sisters. Willow and Violet seemed to come from separate planets.

Violet was lightly tanned with straight hair that obeyed gravity. It was thick, brown, and beautiful—Bumpus hair, the same hair their mom, Aunt Rosie, and Aunt Deenie all had.

Willow, on the other hand, was generally pink (growing steadily pinker throughout the summer), with hair that obeyed no rules. Aside from sharing her dad's freckled skin, there was almost nothing about Willow that resembled anyone else in the entire family. Except for her eyes. Willow had eyes just like Grandpa Bumpus. And by some miracle, so did Delia.

"It's remarkable," people would whisper when they first met Delia and Willow together. Their skin was as different as peanut butter from jelly. ("Delia is the smooth and creamy kind," Willow liked to say, "and I'm raspberry preserves—with the seeds.") But their eyes were the same light brown, just like amber.

Having matching eyes made Willow feel like she and Delia were the true sisters in the family. They saw things the same way.

"Closer than cousins, stronger than sisters, bigger than best friends," they liked to say. Willow and Delia were cousins + sisters + best friends, all wrapped up together.

The door from the kitchen swung open just then, and Willow's mom stepped into the dining room sipping a cup of coffee.

"Willow, you're just the person I'm looking for,"

she began. "I want you and Delia to include Sweet William this week. He can't be bothering Mr. Henry and that new caterer, Ms. What's-Her-Name."

"Cat," Willow and Delia said together.

"Sweet William found a cat? You're kidding!"

"No, Aunt Aggie," Delia corrected with a laugh. "The caterer's name is Cat."

Willow's mom took a gulp of her coffee. Then she started feeling around her head until she found one of the pencils she always tucked in her hair.

"Well, that's just the sort of thing I want to avoid. No cats, dogs, or anything of the sort coming back home with us to Chicago. He already unleashed his crickets on dear Mr. Henry's porch!"

Suddenly Sweet William burst through the back door, Bernice panting at his heels to keep up.

"Mr. Henry said there's frogs out by the willow tree," he shouted, showing them a bright red sand pail he must have been planning to use for frog collecting. "Bernice and me are going to catch some!"

Willow's mom groaned, asking Sweet William to

please leave nature right where he found it. But as he raced for the front door, Bernice skidded to a stop, sniffed the air, and then bounded toward the kitchen.

"Cat made bacon, didn't she?" Willow asked, already certain of the answer.

"Get Bernice out of here," Violet ordered, the medals around her neck jangling noisily as she moved. "You know she can't be trusted around bacon. And Cat wants nothing to do with dogs. Or crickets. Or frogs!"

As Willow and Delia helped Sweet William try to coax their furry, bacon-loving friend away from the kitchen, Willow's mom flipped open her notepad.

"Now listen up, because we're all going to be busy this week. Violet and Darlene are joining us for Aunt Rosie's dress fitting today," she began, her pencil ticking things off another list. "Willow, you and Delia don't need to come. Violet and Darlene have developed over the summer, so their gowns need adjusting . . ."

Willow wrinkled her nose at the thought of Violet's and Darlene's changing figures. Delia plugged her fingers in her ears and began singing "La-la-la."

They turned back to Willow's mom.

". . . but you three need to stick together. No wandering, no trouble, no new pets. And please don't let Bernice bother Ms. Cat. She's got cooking to do. We don't want to wind up in the doghouse, you know."

And then she poked her pencil back into her hair and took the stairs, laughing at her own joke.

Eventually Willow and Delia hoisted Bernice onto all four paws and sent her marching out the door with Sweet William. Then they timidly stepped into the kitchen.

Cat was at the stove, her back to them. They shot each other worried looks. Which was going to be worse—entertaining Sweet William and Bernice, or trying to make nice with Cat after yesterday's sour start?

"Y'all have a couple of lah-dee-dahs in the

family, huh?" Cat drawled, her accent thick as oatmeal. "My big sisters were mean as polecats. Noses stuck so high in the air they nearly drowned every time it rained. When my restaurant was the most popular place in Mississippi, they would come in complaining about the long lines. Never did give me a break."

Cat still wasn't facing them, but she sounded almost friendly. Willow's jaw dropped, and Delia clapped her hands silently behind Cat's back. Maybe she wasn't so cranky after all.

"Mr. Henry thinks the moon rises and sets by y'all," Cat continued. And she finally turned around to reveal two plates piled high with bacon, eggs, waffles, and bright berries. "So I thought we should try to make a fresh start."

Willow and Delia grabbed forks and climbed onto two of the tall stools at the wide marble island. As Willow tucked her sun hat into her back pocket, Cat poured cream in her coffee, then sat down across from them. She looked neater today in a crisp white apron, and her glasses made her eyes appear catlike. Her hair was yellow as macaroni, and Willow thought it looked wavy like noodles, too. Cat had seemed like a giant yesterday, her hands enormous and her fingers like sausages. Today she looked gentler. Willow noticed she wore no jewelry. Not a single bracelet, earring, or even a wedding band.

"This breakfast is delicious," Delia began, neatly dabbing at the corners of her mouth with her napkin. "Will you teach us some of your cooking secrets? We're quick learners."

Willow took a few more bites of her waffle and studied Cat's expression. Delia was on to something. If Cat had run her own restaurant—and a popular one, it sounded like—she could really help them impress Aunt Rosie.

"You probably have lots of cooking tricks up your sleeve," Willow said through a mouth full of waffles. "With you on our team, we'll amaze everybody!"

Delia nodded. "You can help us make extra-fancy desserts like cupcakes with sugar crystals, cute little cake pops, maybe a chocolate fountain!"

Cat waved them off like she was shooing mosquitoes.

"I'm in no position to help anybody," she said, her mouth pinched so tight it looked like a raisin. "Now how about you take those buckets off the back porch and go next door to pick me some blueberries? If I have time later, maybe I'll show you how to make a compote."

It was clear Cat just wanted something—anything—to get Delia and Willow out of her kitchen. The cousins reluctantly agreed, and Willow tried to look on the bright side.

"Maybe this is an opening! Everybody has to start somewhere, right?" she whispered hopefully as they carried their plates over to the sink. "It sort of makes us sous-chefs."

But Delia said back in a hushed voice that they couldn't be sous-chefs until they learned how to pronounce it properly.

Or until they knew what a compote was.

Cat Sutherland's
Simple Southern Compote

Ingredients:

3 cups fresh-picked blueberries

⅓ cup sugar

2 tablespoons water

1 tablespoon fresh lemon juice

Directions:

1. Make sure you have an adult's help.

2. Combine all the ingredients in a small saucepan and cook over medium heat until the blueberry skins have popped and the mixture is slightly thickened, about 6 to 8 minutes.

3. Let cool to room temperature before serving.

4. Top off your compote with whipped cream. Or you can use it as a topping: just drizzle it on anything from pancakes to pound cake, French toast to vanilla ice cream.

Makes about 3 cups of compote.

Compote (the word comes from French) is a dessert made of any kind of fruit—apples, pears, apricots, you name it—in sugary syrup. Eat it hot or cold, on its own or as a topping.

Chapter 6
blueberry surprise

The screen door slammed behind them as Delia and Willow grabbed three white buckets and set off for the neighboring yard. Aunt Deenie was doing stretches on the lawn, her bright blue running shoes hard to miss in the morning sunshine. Last summer she always went jogging with Uncle Delvan. But not today, Willow noticed. Grandpa called over a hello from the far end of the porch, where he was playing checkers with Sweet William.

"What did the bumblebee say to the flower?" Grandpa was asking. "Good morning, honey!"

Sweet William squealed with laughter. After all

his years running a flower shop in Chicago, Grandpa had an endless supply of flower jokes. And Sweet William never tired of hearing them.

Bernice let out a gentle woof, her own version of a morning greeting, then went back to staring into Sweet William's red pail. Willow wondered if there were frogs in it—frogs he planned to bring back to Chicago.

"Should Sweet William come with us?" Delia asked. "Like your mom said?"

Willow looked back over her shoulder to study her brother and Grandpa and the checkerboard.

"Nah, he's busy," she decided, tugging her sun hat over her hair again. "We'll get him later."

The cousins walked along the white fence in search of a gate. Sweet-smelling flowers—Willow thought they must be honeysuckle—trailed along with them, their vines woven in and out of the slats of the old fence. The grass on Mr. Henry's side was lush and green like a carpet, so soft that Willow couldn't resist the urge to kick off her flip-flops and walk barefoot. When they stepped into the yard on the other side, however, it became clear how different the two properties were. The grass was growing in clumps, and the whole yard was dense with bushes and vines extending willy-nilly. It looked wild and a little dangerous.

"This place gives me the creeps," said Delia with a shudder. "Are you sure Cat meant here?"

"Pretty sure," Willow said. And she pointed at an owl perched on the big FOR SALE sign near the cluttered driveway. The owl's unblinking eyes were watching them.

Cat had explained that the blueberry bushes could be found in a thicket at the far side of the property, where the yard ended and the bluff down to the beach began. So the girls skirted the edge of the grounds, keeping their distance from the eerie back porch of the old house.

It had seen better days, that was for sure. Willow couldn't stop turning back to look at the peeling yellow paint and broken steps. A rusty sign propped up near a thick tree in the yard read ART GALLERY in pale blue letters.

Willow stopped suddenly, banging the buckets together.

"It just hit me, Delia. Mr. Henry calls this the old Sutherland place. Isn't that how he introduced Cat yesterday? As Catherine Sutherland? Do you think this place is hers?"

"I've never heard it called anything but ugly," said Delia, looking around. "We haven't met a single Sutherland in all the summers we've come here. Who are they? And what's she doing cooking for Mr. Henry if she has her own house next door?"

Delia and Willow walked on, picking their way past brambles and sharp twigs in search of blueberries. Willow noticed there was no wooden staircase down to the beach like there was at Whispering Pines. It must have rotted away long ago.

They kept a safe distance from the bluff's edge, but Willow could hear the waves on the shore below. The cousins stopped now and then to look west at

the endless blue water. Willow squinted, trying to see Chicago's forest of skyscrapers rising up on the other side of Lake Michigan.

After pushing aside more brambles and tangled vines, Willow let out a gasp. "This must be it. Delia, look!"

They had finally stumbled upon the bushes Cat had promised. Long rows of blueberries were growing wild and undisturbed. It seemed like they'd struck gold—there must have been a million berries waiting to be picked. But Delia suddenly grew cautious.

"We shouldn't touch these," she warned. "They could be poisonous. What if they're not blueberries at all, but something deadly?"

Willow poked her hand through the bushes, examining the berries closely. "Poisonous? What did they teach you at zoo camp? Didn't you tell me that rhyme, 'Leaves of three, let them be'?"

"You don't have to go to zoo camp to know that one," Delia replied, backing away from the berry bushes. "Or to know that we shouldn't just go around eating things we stumble across in the weeds."

Willow couldn't help but laugh at sensible Delia's worries. She popped a blueberry into her mouth, grinning at her cousin as she chewed. Delia did not look amused.

"I brought along my first-aid kit," Delia said, folding her arms across her chest. "It will help if you cut your finger, but it can't do anything if you're poisoned."

Willow began to toss berries into the air and catch them in her mouth like a trained seal. *"Ta-da!"*

"You can be that way," Delia said, squaring her shoulders and using her clear, calm crossing-guard voice again. "But I am going to be smart about this and get out of here."

Willow shrugged and tried to look casual. "Go if you want," she teased, "but you'll have to walk past the creepy house all alone."

That did the trick. Delia turned back toward the bushes, sniffed at a berry, and gave it a hesitant nibble.

She seemed to accept that it was a fruit she knew.

The girls got to work, and as the hot August sun beat down on the two busy heads—one covered in a broad blue sun hat, the other in braided pigtails—their buckets began to fill. They had very different techniques for picking. Delia developed a precise one-handed method for freeing just the plumpest berries, holding the bucket securely in her other hand. She said the blueberries reminded her of jewelry, dangling earrings made of big, round sapphires.

Willow had her own way of going about it. She wedged her bucket into the bushes just below the biggest clusters, then ran both her hands over the berries and tickled them off the stems. She made sure to pluck only the deep blue ones and leave the green berries still attached. They dropped into the bucket with a satisfying thumping sound. Her method was faster than Delia's, but her bucket spilled twice.

"Hey, what is that?" Willow called out. Now it seemed to be her turn to worry.

"What are you talking about?" asked Delia, who

had disappeared into a particularly thick bush.

Willow stood still as a garden gnome.

"That flapping thing," she said, her voice dripping with panic. "It's right beside me! Is it a bat? What if it's a vampire bat? What if it wants to suck my blood?"

Delia poked her head up. A shape hovered in the air between them. It darted in and out of the patches of sunlight that broke through the trees. Willow saw red, green, white.

"Oh, Willow!" Delia whispered. "It's not a bat. Stay perfectly still so you don't scare them off."

Willow let out a whimper.

"Them?"

"They're hummingbirds. We've stirred up a nest or something. Look how beautiful they are!"

Four or five tiny creatures were flitting in the air. Once Willow could breathe again, she relaxed and watched the fairylike figures hover here and there over the blueberry bushes.

"You don't have to worry about them sucking

your blood," Delia whispered. "Maybe they'll shower you with pixie dust instead."

Willow grinned and stayed rooted to the spot. And in whispered agreement, both girls decided they really did like nature, so long as it didn't bite, sting, poison them, or get tangled in their hair. She and Delia spent the next long while standing quiet as trees and drinking in the magical world they'd discovered.

The old Sutherland place was starting to seem a lot less creepy.

"I think hummingbirds are good luck, too," Delia

said in hushed excitement. "I read it in a book about the Zuni Indians. They believed hummingbirds helped them overcome the impossible."

Overcome the impossible. Willow liked the sound of that. Even though she was a little fuzzy on the Zuni, she figured hummingbirds had to be lucky. The way they could fly backward and hover in the air made them special, not to mention their glittery feathers.

Eventually the birds moved on and the three buckets grew heavy. The cousins decided to head back to Whispering Pines, putting the fullest bucket between them and sharing the load. But just as they reached the white fence, Willow heard a strange honking sound and faint barking in the distance.

"Oh, no! That's got to be Sweet William!"

They ran the length of the wooden fence, trying their best not to spill the precious blueberries in the process, until they found the gate.

"It's coming from the vegetable garden, over there," Delia said, nodding toward the far side of the property.

They set their buckets beside the nearest tree.
Willow took off, running barefoot through the grass
while Delia flip-flopped behind her. When they
reached the garden, it quickly became clear what the
honking was about.

There was Sweet
William, face-to-face
with an angry Canada
goose. Willow had never

been that close to one, and it was surprisingly large. And feisty, too, hissing and snapping at Sweet William, who was standing his ground and growling like a bear.

Neither goose nor boy seemed ready to back down.

"Do something, Willow!" urged Delia. "Try one of your karate moves!"

Willow didn't think she could karate chop a goose, even if it was threatening her little brother.

"Get out of here, you bully!" she shouted, flapping her arms. Delia joined in, and they looked like a pair of angry exotic birds.

When he heard them, Sweet William spun around in surprise. The goose decided to strike, nipping the index finger of his left hand. Then, as if it thought Sweet William might bite back, the goose flapped away.

"It's all right,

Sweet William," Willow soothed, pulling him into a hug. Delia pointed to what had probably caused the whole commotion. It was a round, white goose egg, nestled snugly in the leaves beneath some broccoli plants.

"That was a mama goose," Delia explained, running a hand through Sweet William's mop of curly brown hair. "She was protecting her baby. Like Aunt Aggie protects you."

"And Bernice," he sniffled. "Bernice protects me, too. Usually."

Willow felt a twinge of guilt that she hadn't been watching after her little brother. But it passed as quickly as it came, and she moved on to wondering where Bernice had gone.

Her answer came in the form of more honking. Willow, Delia, and Sweet William all looked up just in time to see Bernice race past the other end of the garden, the angry goose nipping at her tail.

Sweet William shook off Willow's arm and dove through the green web of cucumber vines. He snapped off a particularly long cucumber and waved it like a knight's sword, then dashed across the yard to rescue Bernice. Delia raced after him, only she tip-toed carefully through the jalapeño peppers. Just as Willow stood up to follow, something caught her eye.

It was Mr. Henry, crouched in the shade beside some tomato bushes down a nearby row. He was pulling bright red ones from a vine and tucking them suspiciously under his straw hat and into the pockets of his shirt.

Willow couldn't help but wonder: If Mr. Henry was the owner of Whispering Pines, why was he sneaking around in his own garden?

It must have been only ten minutes later, though it felt much longer to Willow, when they collected their buckets of blueberries from the yard and filed into the kitchen. Thankfully, there was not a goose in sight. Nor a Cat.

"Let's get that finger cleaned up," Willow said, fanning her pink cheeks to cool down.

"And don't forget Bernice's tail," Sweet William added.

Delia pulled out her first-aid kit from the pocket of her shorts and popped it open. She laid bandages, gauze, and a goopy ointment on the counter before them and got to work on her little cousin's finger.

Once she finished with Sweet William, Delia delicately wrapped Bernice's tail. Willow and Sweet William stared in silent awe, their jaws hanging open.

"You really do carry a first-aid kit with you!" exclaimed Willow in amazement. "All I have in my pockets is the lucky penny and a lint-covered peppermint."

"The way you took such good care of Bernice," Sweet William whispered, "you're like a vegetarian."

"I think you mean *veterinarian*," Delia said with a smile. "And thanks. I am pretty good, aren't I?"

Willow helped Sweet William down from the kitchen stool. And while she was grateful for her cousin's care, Willow couldn't shake the feeling that everybody in the family seemed to have something they were good at—except her.

Chapter 7
things don't always
go smoothie

Once enough bandages, hugs, and belly rubs had been administered, Delia ushered her patients out of the kitchen. Willow found Sweet William's container of modeling clay and set him up on the porch near Grandpa, where he could make the people he called the Clay Family. Bernice lay down at his feet, keeping what Willow figured was a sharp lookout for Mother Goose.

Back in the kitchen, the cousins hoisted the buckets onto the counter and began washing some of the fruit. With so many fresh blueberries, Willow and Delia decided this was a perfect opportunity to show

Aunt Rosie what they could do in the kitchen. And what better way to impress Cat, too, while they were at it?

"We could make a pie," suggested Delia. "Everybody likes pie, right?"

"That would take too long," Willow said, wiping at a bead of sweat on her forehead. "Grandpa said Cat went to the bank. We have no idea when she's coming back."

"Let's put together a cobbler," Delia offered. "They're fast."

Willow tugged on her T-shirt and tried to cool off. "Hey, I've got it. Today is so hot—why don't we make blueberry ice cream? Or even faster, let's make ice-cold smoothies!"

Willow pointed over to the back of the kitchen, where an old-fashioned silver blender sat on the countertop. It was gleaming in the bright morning, like it was winking at them to come on over.

"That's great," Delia agreed. "I'll grab ice and some yogurt, and you finish washing the berries."

The cousins got busy, looking like a couple of

professional chefs. They spooned in the yogurt. They dropped in the blueberries. They shook in the ice. Delia and Willow were just seconds away from a cool, refreshing treat, confident their smoothies would amaze anyone who was lucky enough to get a sip.

"Aunt Rosie will love these," Delia said. She measured just the right amount of honey, then poked down the ingredients with her spoon. "We're on our way to kissing those flower-girl dresses good-bye!"

"And when Cat tastes them, she'll see how amazing we are! Then she'll help us cook for the wedding." Willow smiled as she set the lid on top and flipped the switch. "Good-bye, pink!"

But it was more like *Hello, purple.*

Whirr, zzzupp, then *POW!*

The lid shot off like a rocket. And smoothie followed. Bluish-purple slush spattered the white kitchen walls, splattering the wide-eyed cousins in fruity goo.

"Oh, no!" shouted Delia, covering her now-purple face with her hands.

"Shut it off!" screeched Willow, whose hair had turned a light purple.

"You do it!"

"I can't find it!"

Both girls' hands reached the switch at the same time. And in the heavy silence that followed the noisy whirring, neither cousin so much as breathed. When Willow finally looked at Delia, a laugh burst out of her chest and sounded like the blender itself. Delia snorted with laughter too, sticking out a finger and scooping smoothie off Willow's cheek.

"Delicious," Delia managed through hysterical hiccups, "and so refreshing!"

Thwack!

The screen door smacked shut, and there was Cat, standing in the doorway with Mr. Henry.

". . . so handy around here," she was saying, "I wanted to see if you could fix my old blender. . . ."

Willow and Delia jumped as if Cat had poked them both with a hot spatula. They began racing in every direction, grabbing paper towels and

dishrags and anything they could get their hands on that might clean up the purple gunk.

Mr. Henry and Cat were completely silent, standing there dumbfounded as the girls frantically cleaned. And it wasn't until Willow was running a cloth over the white tiles along the wall that she noticed a piece of paper taped to the back of the blender. She nudged Delia to take a look, too. And wiping away a blob of mushed blueberry, they read the words:

NEEDS FIXING! DO NOT TOUCH!

Willow & Delia's Delightfully Delicious Blueberry Smoothie

Ingredients:

1 cup low-fat vanilla yogurt

1 cup fresh-picked blueberries

2 tablespoons honey

2 cups ice

Directions:

1. Make sure you have an adult's help.

2. Pour all the ingredients into a blender, saving the ice for last so it doesn't lock up the blender's blades.

3. Make sure the lid is on tight so you don't redecorate your kitchen.

4. Flip the switch and blend it all together. You might have to turn the blender off, poke the ice around with a long spoon, then blend some more.

5. Don't forget to hold the lid on tight!

6. Blend again until all the ingredients are mixed smoothly together. Be sure all the ice chunks are broken up.

7. Drink up and cool down!

Makes about 4 cups of smoothie.

You can make a smoothie from just about any fruit. Look around your kitchen and decide what might taste best. Try combining flavors, like strawberry-banana or peach-raspberry.

Chapter 8
roasting marshmallows

*l*ater that evening, once dinner was finished and the sun was setting, Willow and Delia wanted to put a little distance between themselves and Cat's kitchen. So they organized a marshmallow roast for Aunt Rosie on the beach, using the fancy treats packed from home. Grandpa agreed to help out.

"This is the right time to bring out all her favorite snacks," Willow plotted, lugging her polka-dotted bag across the sand. "Then we'll pitch our plan to make desserts for the wedding. I can show her the recipes I've collected in my notebook."

Delia agreed. "And even though we made a mess

with the smoothie, it still tasted delicious! She's bound to like our cooking."

"What do you call a flower that makes a mess?" asked Grandpa as he dragged a long piece of driftwood over to the fire ring. "An *oopsy*-daisy!"

Willow couldn't help but laugh. No matter what problems anyone in the family faced, Grandpa

and Grandma both believed flowers could make everything all right. Willow figured it came from all the years running their flower shop, Bumpus Blooms. The two of them were flower obsessed.

Then, as she pulled her recipe notebook from the dotted bag and flipped through a few pages, Willow wondered if she was a little obsessed, too—with desserts instead of daffodils.

"Yoo-hoo! Is there room for more at your campfire?"

Suddenly Grandma appeared on the staircase, waving at them with her green-garden-gloved hands and marching down the steep wooden steps from the house. Behind her followed the whole Bumpus family, looking a lot like a circus parade. Bernice, who was wearing a collar of braided daisies, let out an excited woof when she spotted Willow.

"Grandma took some flowers from the garden," gushed Sweet William once he and Bernice reached the fire. "She's making daisy shames for us to wear."

Willow's dad adjusted his own crown of yellow

blooms and told Sweet William it was a daisy *chain*, not a daisy *shame*.

"But Mr. Henry said it was a shame Grandma cut so many of his flowers," Sweet William protested.

Willow's dad pressed his finger to his lips to shush Sweet William. Then he unfurled a blanket and helped Grandma take a seat. She plunked down a wicker basket filled with fresh blooms and offered to weave a circle of daisies for Willow and Delia.

"How are we doing, darlings?" she said, her fingers beginning to work a few daisy stems. "You've had an eventful day, I believe."

Willow and Delia shot each other nervous looks. They weren't sure how many family members knew about their smoothie disaster.

"We're great, Grandma," Willow said with a bounce. "Just excited to roast marshmallows with Aunt Rosie. We have a few things to talk to her about."

"Important things," added Delia with a serious nod.

Grandma stopped her daisy braiding and eyed

them suspiciously. "Yes, as Rosie's flower girls, you are an important part of her wedding. I'm sure you understand that."

Willow couldn't help feeling that Grandma was trying to tell them something. But she shrugged her shoulders. Making amazing desserts for Aunt Rosie's wedding was important, too. Once Grandma tasted their cupcakes and tarts, she'd understand how their talents were being wasted as flower girls.

"Make our chains next, Grandma," interrupted Violet, who took a seat with Darlene on the blanket beside their grandmother. "I can pretend mine is a victory wreath I win at the Olympics."

Willow elbowed Delia and rolled her eyes.

"I wore a crown of flowers when I danced *The Nutcracker* last Christmas," added Darlene. "I was the Sugar Plum Fairy. You know, the star."

Now it was Delia's turn to roll her eyes.

There was no getting away from big sisters and their amazing accomplishments, even at the beach.

Just then Aunt Rosie stepped into the circle

gathered around the campfire. Delia scooped up a container of Mentos in one hand and a box of Good & Plenty in the other, while Willow tore into the package of fancy marshmallows. This was their big moment to win her over.

"Girls, it is so sweet of you to organize this," Aunt Rosie began, nibbling on the marshmallow Willow handed her. Eyeing Delia's offerings, she added, "Somehow you know exactly what I love to eat."

"Let's just say we do our homework," Delia said slyly, pouring a handful of pink and white candies into her aunt's palm. "Willow and I would like to talk to you . . ."

Suddenly Delia got tongue-tied. She looked at Willow for help.

". . . talk to you . . ." Willow continued, her eyes darting from Delia to her aunt, "about other things you love to eat! Like at your wedding! We don't want to . . ."

And now Willow was the one with her tongue in a knot. She looked desperately at Delia. One of them had to tell Aunt Rosie what they had wanted to say all summer.

"We don't want to tiptoe around this anymore—" Delia blurted.

"Did you hear that?" giggled Aunt Rosie to Jonathan, who was standing beside her holding what looked like two miniature guitars. "They said *tiptoe!*"

And she let out a happy squeak that sounded like a baby bird. Jonathan grinned and handed one of the instruments to Aunt Rosie. They both began strumming the tiny strings.

"Aren't these adorable?" she asked Delia and Willow. "They're ukuleles. Jonathan and I took lessons so we could perform at the wedding!"

And off they scampered like a couple of gleeful squirrels. Before Willow could collect herself and start passing out the marshmallows for roasting, Aunt Rosie and Jonathan were already on the second verse of "Tiptoe Through the Tulips." Grandpa and Grandma were singing along with them, arms around each other on the blanket and rocking side to side. Willow's parents joined in, too, along with Sweet William and Aunt Deenie.

"Oh, tiptoe from the garden, by the garden of the willow tree . . ."

Willow sneaked a glance beside her at Delia. Her cousin was staring openmouthed across the fire at Violet and Darlene, who were joyfully belting out the lyrics with Uncle Delvan. Even Bernice got swept up in it all, turning her face toward the sky and howling along in a moonlight serenade, Bumpus family style.

"Tiptoe through the tulips with meeeeeeeeee!"

Before long, Mr. Henry joined their noisy,

singing circle on the beach. He offered his usual polite nods to everyone as he passed, then took a spot at the log where Willow and Delia were seated. He stuck a marshmallow on a long roasting stick.

"Judging from those buckets in the kitchen, it looks like you two picked the blueberry bushes clean," he said gently, his voice just loud enough to be heard over the ukuleles and the rest of the family's crooning. "But I would stay clear of the kitchen for a while, if I were you."

Delia cringed, and Willow tried to think of something else to talk about besides spattered smoothies. Right away she recalled blueberry picking at the creepy old house next door to Whispering Pines. And she began asking Mr. Henry to tell them all about it.

"Is it Cat Sutherland's?" asked Delia, making sure to keep her marshmallow from the flame. "Does she live there now?"

"Is it haunted?" Willow wondered. "Full of ghosts?"

After a few minutes of begging, Mr. Henry finally

agreed to spill some of the beans about the old yellow house. The girls sat in silence as he got going, afraid that if they interrupted, he'd leave them with more questions than answers.

"Ms. Catherine is indeed the owner of that property," he began, his face a pale orange in the fire-light. "It belonged to her great-aunt, who died a few years back."

And then Mr. Henry seemed lost in his own thoughts, his voice low. Willow and Delia leaned in closer so they wouldn't miss a word.

"Cat had never set foot in Michigan before October. She lived her whole life down South," he said, rotating the marshmallow he was roasting. "But things went bad with her restaurant a few years ago. The way I heard it, some theme restaurants moved in. You know the kind—one served French food and had its own Eiffel Tower salad bar. Another one served Greek food, with the waiters wearing togas. Folks down there went crazy for them, and they left Cat's restaurant behind."

Mr. Henry shook his head, making a *tsk-tsk* sound. Then he blew on his marshmallow to put out the flame. Willow and Delia examined theirs, pulling them away from the fire when they had turned a gooey, golden brown.

"Everyone else in Cat's family is dead now. She's alone in the world. So that run-down old house next door is all she has left. Period." Mr. Henry licked the charred marshmallow off his fingers. "That and whatever money she makes cooking at Whispering Pines. But it's not enough. Ms. Catherine needs to build up her catering business. She needs to reach more people."

Delia shuddered, and Willow didn't think it was from the night breeze.

"I feel awful for her," Delia said, looking up toward the bluff, where Whispering Pines stood like a dollhouse on a shelf. "It sounds as bad as what my dad is going through. It's scary to lose your job. How are you supposed to pay for things? How do you buy food or clothes? How are you supposed to live?"

Willow shifted on the log. "Is that why she's selling the place? Why she's got the big For Sale sign up?"

Mr. Henry was quiet as he poked two more marshmallows onto his roasting stick. Delia and Willow nibbled on theirs.

"She doesn't want to sell it. The house has been in the Sutherland family for generations," Mr. Henry continued. "But the bank is making her, inviting developers to come tear it down. Sure, it needs some work—the gutters are full of leaves, it's got broken steps inside and out, shingles are missing off the roof. But it's not a wreck. They want to knock it down and build a row of condominiums."

Willow popped her gooey marshmallow into her mouth and gazed up toward the blueberry thicket, as if she could see the delicate hummingbirds they'd met that morning. Now a chill ran up her spine.

What would happen to the hummingbirds if their nests were torn down?

"Cat says it'll happen over her dead body," Mr. Henry added. "But it's getting to a point where she won't have any choice."

Chapter 9
a run-through

The next morning, Delia's and Willow's feet had just reached the bottom step of the staircase when the girls bumped into their mothers.

"Deenie took me"—*pant, pant*—"jogging"—*pant, pant*—"down on the beach," Willow's mom was trying to explain. Then she added, with a serious nod, "Healthy."

Willow didn't think the green tinge to her mother's cheeks looked so healthy, but she decided not to comment.

"Girls, the big day is almost here," Aunt Deenie began, wiping a drop of sweat from her forehead but

otherwise looking unfazed by their exercise. "And you know how organized Rosie is. She wants to have a rehearsal. *This morning*. So we need everyone in his or her place in the yard to run through the wedding ceremony."

Finally able to breathe normally, Willow's mom tried to join in. "Mr. Henry's brother, Reverend Roland Rickles, will be here in a half hour," she said with a few puffs, feeling around her hair in search of a hidden pencil. "And so will Jonathan's entire family from the green B and B down the road. So you girls need flower baskets in your hands and thinking caps on your heads."

Willow rolled her eyes. Did her mom have to sound like a librarian even on vacation?

Aunt Deenie said something about wedding hairdos, and she began sweeping Willow's unruly curls into a pile on top of her head. Delia let out a laugh, until Aunt Deenie told her that she was next.

"There," Aunt Deenie announced, stepping back from Willow like she'd just fixed a leaky faucet.

"Much better, don't you think, Aggie?"

"She looks darling," cooed Willow's mom. "Like a perfect flower girl. We'll do this hairstyle for the wedding Saturday, and clip pink roses and ribbons all around the bun."

The bun?

Willow threw her hands to her head, patting around until she touched the towering mound. It felt like a bird's nest was perched up there. Did she look like a bubblehead? Like some fancy beauty-pageant girl? What would her karate class say if they saw her like this?

"And we can do a bun for you, too," Aunt Deenie beamed, reaching for Delia's braids. "With matching hairstyles and matching dresses, you girls will look adorable."

There it was again, that word: *adorable*.

"No way. Never. *Uh-uh*," Delia said under her breath.

Willow didn't want to look adorable either. She wanted to escape. Tugging on Delia's arm, she announced that they were going to search for Sweet William.

"Tell him it's time to get his hair brushed for the rehearsal," Willow's mom called after them. "On second thought, don't mention the brush. . . ."

Willow and Delia checked the garden and the porch. But it wasn't until they heard a muffled croaking sound in the upstairs hallway that they decided to look in his room. Sweet William was under the bed.

"We've got to talk," Willow said, tugging at her hair and freeing her curls. "Aunt Rosie wants to practice for the wedding. But you can't have another run-in with that goose in front of everybody."

Sweet William scrambled out from under the bed, pushing an open cardboard box that served as a home for his frogs. Bernice gave them a protective sniff, then wagged her tail approvingly.

"It's all right," Sweet William said. "Bernice and me have it all worked out. We told Dad I was too nervous to practice for the wedding, so Bernice is going to do it for me."

Bernice perked up her ears and watched the doorway, letting them know someone was coming. It allowed just enough time for Sweet William to slide the frog box out of view before Uncle Delvan popped his head into the room.

"What's with all the serious faces?" he asked, tugging worriedly at his goatee. "Is something wrong?"

All three cousins sprang to their feet. The last thing they needed was for a grown-up to discover Sweet William's new pets. Willow sniffed the air, wondering whether Uncle Delvan would be able to identify the grimy frog odor she was smelling.

"Nothing's wrong, Dad," Delia was saying, pushing him across the hall toward the room she shared with Willow. "In fact, we were just goofing around. Right, you guys?"

Willow and Sweet William agreed loudly that they were, indeed, goofing. And to prove it, Willow picked up one of Sweet William's stuffed animals—a green turtle—and hurled it from her brother's bedroom across the hall. Delia turned around just in time, and it smacked her squarely on the forehead as if hitting a bull's-eye.

Delia snorted and picked it up, flinging it right back at Willow. Only she hit the wrong cousin. The turtle whacked Sweet William in the chest and sent him collapsing to the floor in a fit of giggles. Willow scooped up all the stuffed animals she could find on his bed and raced past Sweet William into her and Delia's bedroom, shouting, "Fort war!"

Willow and Delia dove for cover on the far side

of the room, behind Delia's bed. Sweet William and Uncle Delvan ducked behind Willow's, quickly gathering up flip-flops, T-shirts, and decorative pillows—anything they could find that would make a good projectile. Even Bernice was barking excitedly, having participated in plenty of these battles over the years.

"Take that!" hollered Uncle Delvan as he shot a balled-up pair of socks across the room at Delia. They nicked her right ear.

Willow fired back with a beanbag penguin, grazing him on the arm. Sweet William lobbed a lacy pillow at the girls like it was a grenade. It thumped Willow on the head, and the room erupted with laughter. Delia used two hands and fired off matching teddy bears. One of them hit a lamp beside Willow's bed, and the other nearly knocked Uncle Delvan right in the nose.

The fort war raged on until they heard Willow's dad calling from downstairs. Sweet William dashed back into his room and under the bed as Uncle Delvan led the girls—Willow, Delia, and Bernice—down-stairs for the rehearsal.

"Flower girls!" Aunt Rosie ordered, sounding more like a Chicago traffic cop than a blushing bride-to-be. "You go down the aisle first."

Delia stared across the yard at Aunt Rosie and confessed in a hushed voice to Willow, "I forgot my rose-petal basket in Detroit. How much trouble do you think I'm in?"

"About as much as I'm in," Willow said with a sheepish grin. "I left mine in Chicago."

"But we have to carry something down the aisle," Delia said. "What should we do?"

Willow peered over at Violet and Darlene. They were already in line for their turn in the procession, carrying gorgeous bouquets of flowers gathered from the yard. They looked as if they'd stepped right out of an oil painting in a museum.

"What do you call a country where everyone drives pink cars?" asked Grandpa, adding sprigs of honeysuckle to Violet's bouquet. Then, with a wink in Willow and Delia's direction, he answered, "A pink carnation!"

Willow winked back, then watched Grandpa as he handed Grandma a single red zinnia before he headed off to his place in line.

It was time to start the rehearsal! What were she and Delia going to carry? Delia was so worried about the missing baskets she was chewing on her braids again. Willow decided to slip over to the vegetable garden, where she snapped off a cluster of bright orange peppers from an overflowing plant.

"What do you think of these?" she asked Delia. "Maybe they're silly enough to make everyone forget about the baskets."

"Perfect," Delia sighed with relief. Then she gathered a bouquet of cherry tomatoes for herself. "And we can make Aunt Rosie a salad when we're done!"

Jonathan was all smiles as they walked down the aisle toward him. He plucked a tomato from Delia's bouquet and popped it into his mouth as they took their places on the bride's side of the aisle. Uncle Delvan and Willow's dad were already standing on the groom's side next to Jonathan's brothers, Peter and Kevin.

The rest of the rehearsal was uneventful, even with Bernice trotting down the aisle as a stand-in for Sweet William. Willow tried to pay attention to Reverend Roland as he explained the details for the actual wedding ceremony, but all she could think about were awful pink dresses.

Suddenly, the familiar sound of growling snapped Willow back.

"Sweet William, no!" Delia was shouting.

"I thought he was under the bed," Willow moaned. "He must have sneaked out to watch!"

Her little brother came tearing down the aisle, roaring like an angry bear and waving a particularly long

cucumber like he was a swashbuckling swordsman. A green vine that must have been a cucumber plant was caught on his shirt and trailed behind him like a streamer from a St. Patrick's Day parade.

He was running to get away from Mother Goose, who was honking and hissing and snapping her beak in hot pursuit, clearly upset about this featherless, curly-haired creature who had come too close to her egg. Bernice caught sight of a loved one in distress, so she took off after Sweet William and the goose, seemingly thrilled by the excitement of the whole scene.

"Never a dull moment with the Bumpus family, is there?" Jonathan asked, planting a kiss on Aunt Rosie's cheek. His parents, brothers, and the entire groom's side of the aisle were covering their mouths, attempting to keep their smiles from the pink-cheeked bride and her red-faced sisters. But those sisters

were already on the case, pushing straight over toward Delia and Willow.

"What in heaven's name is going on?" demanded Aunt Deenie.

Before they could answer, another shout from the end of the aisle had them all turning their heads. It was Cat, wielding a black skillet in her hand and running through the yard after the earlier bandits.

"I've had it with those critters tearing up my garden and stealing my vegetables," Cat snarled, waving the skillet over her head like a Statue of Liberty gone mad.

"Willow Antonia Sweeney," her mom began, a long pause hanging in the air as she watched Cat storm down the aisle. "What is your little brother doing running through here with a duck?"

Willow and Delia hid their vegetable bouquets behind their backs.

"Not to get technical, Aunt Aggie," Delia pointed out, "but that was a Canada goose, not a duck."

It was late afternoon when Grandma and Grandpa

started the slow climb up the bluff staircase from the beach, Delia and Willow behind them. The girls had made sure to bring Sweet William and Bernice along, just for safekeeping.

"If we get into more trouble with Cat," Willow had whispered, "then our goose is cooked. And maybe even our dog."

"It should be that Mother Goose," added Delia.

Now their mothers were waiting for them on the back porch. Willow's stomach did a little flip. This did not look good.

"You girls can go straight to your bedroom for the rest of the day," Willow's mom said in a tight voice. "It will give you time to reflect on your actions."

"We've just learned what's been going on," Aunt Deenie added, her voice as clipped as her sister's. "What were you girls thinking?"

Neither Willow nor Delia dared to speak. What exactly were their moms talking about?

Were they upset about the goose?

Or the vegetable garden?

Sweet William's frogs?

The blueberry-spatter smoothies?

The salty lemonade?

Or did their moms finally realize how much Delia and Willow were trying to get out of being flower girls?

"We didn't mean to make anybody mad," the cousins protested timidly. "We're sorry for . . ."

And then Willow remembered the missing flower-petal baskets. Was *that* what had their mothers so upset?

Willow wasn't sure which crime they were being punished for, and from the look of it, neither did Delia. But as their mothers tsk-tsked and pointed fingers toward the door, Willow was a little impressed by one thing.

Never in her life had she had such a long list of possibilities.

Chapter 10
good morning, sunshine

are you awake?"

"Yes, I've been awake for a while," answered Delia in the darkness. "I can't sleep. I hate being in trouble."

"Me too," said Willow. "But we haven't done anything wrong, really. It's not fair that we're the ones getting punished. Sweet William loves animals. Is that our fault? Plus Violet and Darlene are oldest. They should be the ones watching after him instead of us."

"And the salty lemonade," began Delia. "It's not like we meant for that to happen."

"Or for the smoothie to explode," added Willow.

Delia agreed. It didn't feel fair.

"But today's a new day," she said, sitting on the side of her creaky bed. "The sun isn't even up yet. We could go see it rise. I've never done that before."

Willow thought it sounded like a great idea. But her body just needed a bit more convincing to get out of bed. She peeked over at the clock on the square bedside table between them. It read 5:28.

"Why is it called the *crack* of dawn? Maybe they should name it the *pop* of dawn," she yawned, snuggling deeper into her pillow, "because it probably just sort of pops up like a jack-in-the-box. Or if it's slower than that, maybe the *inch* of dawn?"

"If you'd get up, Sleeping Beauty, we could go see for ourselves," Delia whispered, tugging on Willow's flowery quilt. She tossed a few Mentos in her mouth, then poured some into Willow's hand.

"I'm good," Willow said, finally sitting up and pushing stray curls from her eyes. She blinked a few times, trying to focus. How had Delia already made her bed? "Okay, let's go."

Throwing on fresh shorts, T-shirts, and hoodies, the cousins pushed open their creaky door and headed out into the hall. They decided carrying their flip-flops might make for a quieter escape, but Bernice heard them anyway. She greeted them with a few sniffs and sleepy wags before circling back into Sweet William's room and flopping down on a pile of pillows beside his bed.

As they sneaked down the hall, Willow held tight to Delia, who was leading the way with a yellow flashlight she'd brought from home.

"I can't see when you're in front," Willow whispered as they tried to descend the staircase without tripping on each other. "Can't we both hold it?"

Delia made room on the step for Willow to join her, and they wrapped their hands around the flashlight's long handle and tried not to fall down the stairs, all while suppressing the urge to giggle wildly.

Silently shutting the front door behind them,

the girls stepped onto the chilly porch. When Delia clicked off the flashlight, their sunrise adventure suddenly seemed dangerous. They were going out into the yard? Where it was still very, very dark?

Giddy and giggling and stumbling onto the lawn, Willow and Delia gazed up into the thick blue blanket above them. The moon had set, but the sky was still lit with stars. Delia even pointed out a constellation. "It's called Ursa Major," she said. "It means Big Bear—grrrrrrr!"

Delia lunged at Willow, sending both of them screeching and laughing and deeper into the dark yard. There was something exhilarating about being outside so early, when everyone else was still asleep.

That is, almost everyone else.

Willow noticed a faint light on the far side of the property. It was shining through the one small window of Mr. Henry's hobby shed.

"Look over there, Delia," she whispered, pointing in the shed's direction. "What do you think Mr. Henry could possibly be doing in there at this hour?"

But just as Delia turned toward the shed, the light went out.

"What are you talking about, Willow?"

"Someone is in there," Willow said, pressing in a little closer toward her cousin on the wet grass. She tried to remember some of her karate moves, just in case. "I swear that light was on not two seconds ago."

"Or maybe you're seeing ghosts," Delia teased.

Willow squinted into the darkness, wondering if her eyes were playing tricks on her. Ghosts at Whispering Pines? Ha, she told herself, but she made sure to cling tightly to the edge of her cousin's sweat-shirt. More like Mr. Henry is up to something again, just like he was yesterday in the garden with those tomatoes.

Once the cousins stopped squirming, the night noises picked back up again. The whir of the crick-ets grew louder, as if an unseen hand had turned up the volume. The frogs joined in, their creaking calls punctuating the crickets' hum like they were carrying on separate conversations across the yard. Which Willow guessed they were.

"Does it look brighter over there?" Delia asked, pointing to the east.

The problem with "over there" was that a whole lot of trees were blocking their view. Whispering Pines teetered on the absolute edge of western Michigan, so watching the sun sink down into the water each evening was easy. Nothing blocked the view west as far as the eye could see. But looking east? That was tricky.

"You'll have to move to higher ground to see the

sun come up," said a voice behind them, "if that's what you're doing out here."

Both girls screamed, and the flashlight flew out of Delia's hand.

Uncle Delvan stepped off the front porch, his laughter and shushing doing nothing to calm their shrieks for the first few moments until they collected themselves. Then Willow's dad came around from the back of the house, shining his own bright flashlight at the three of them.

"What are you doing out here?" he called.

"Us? It's more like what are *you* doing out here?" Willow gasped, her emotions so jumbled up that she wanted to cry and burst out in hysterical laughter at the same time. "You scared us to death!"

"*We* scared *you*?" said Uncle Delvan, running his hand through his goatee and looking exasperated. "I heard creaking on the stairs and got up to investigate. I thought I'd find a bear visiting for the wedding."

More thoughts of bears in the yard sent the cousins into fits of laughter again.

"The giggling woke me up," added Willow's dad, flicking off his flashlight. "From the sound of it, I expected a goose was waddling around the living room."

Stifling another laugh, Delia pointed out that geese didn't giggle. They honked.

"But the real question," said Uncle Delvan, "is what are you two doing out here in the yard when you should be in your room?"

Both Willow and Delia erupted at the same time with explanations and apologies, along with lots of squirming and giggling. Uncle Delvan tried to quiet them, saying he was happy they were celebrating the wonders of nature, but could they please find a more reasonable hour to do it? "Like after nine in the morning?"

Finally Willow's dad suggested they go out for breakfast, just the four of them. "You girls have done your time in your room. Delvan and I can let you off—but just don't do it again."

Willow looked at Delia, who was gazing back at

her with a single eyebrow raised. They seemed to ask each other the same question: Don't do *what* again?

Willow wanted to change the subject, fast.

"How about you take us peach picking over at your friend's orchard?" she suggested with a bounce. "The early bird gets the, you know . . . peach! Then we can come home and make peach parfaits for everybody."

Her dad let out a big yawn. He said a plate of scrambled eggs and a hot cup of coffee made at a diner sounded better than having to work for his breakfast. But after Willow's begging and pleading and tugging and hugging, he finally gave in.

"Only if there's a peach crumble in it for me somewhere," he said. Willow crossed her heart and promised to make him a dessert.

"Can we wake Mom to come, too?" Delia asked, timidly turning to her dad. "Mom loves to go peach picking."

Uncle Delvan brushed Delia's cheek with his fingers and shook his head. He said Aunt Deenie was probably going for a morning jog soon—on her own.

Then he and Willow's dad headed for the car.

As Willow slipped on her flip-flops, she noticed Delia had grown quiet. "What's wrong? Don't you want to go?"

Delia wiped at her eyes and looked at the upstairs windows. She shrugged. "I wish my mom and dad liked each other, the way they used to. Then we could act like a family again."

It wasn't too much later when the dads and daughters settled in at an old wooden picnic table to watch the sunrise. They had hopped the fence that surrounded the orchard grounds and used Delia's flashlight to follow a dirt road to a hilltop. Willow's dad said there was no better place for watching the sun come up.

"Did your friend really say we could pick fruit here anytime, Dad?" Willow asked, peach juice running down her chin as she spoke. He and Uncle Delvan were seated on the bench and leaning their backs against the picnic table, each of them taking bites of the peaches they'd just plucked from nearby trees. Willow and Delia were between them, perched on the tabletop and tapping their feet on the wooden bench.

Delia was somehow able to keep from making a mess, but Willow had to wipe her chin with the sleeve of her sweatshirt a few times.

"Yes, he did say anytime," her dad answered with a yawn. "But I don't know if he meant six in the morning."

As they gazed off toward the eastern horizon, a grayish haze hung over the treetops at the far end of the orchard. The sky in the distance was tinted yellow, but directly overhead was still a deep blue. Delia pointed out the last stars that still twinkled. A few puffy, purple clouds drifted to the south—purple, Willow was reminded, like Violet's and Darlene's junior-bridesmaid dresses. She shook her head to clear her mind, then scanned the wide-open sky again. Thank goodness there was no pink.

"Here comes the sun," Delia said softly. "There's just a sliver of orange peeking up."

Willow looped her arm through her cousin's and snuggled in tight. She was hardly ever up this early during the school year, and never during summer vacation. Even though she should have been tired, she was much too excited.

"It looks like a giant peach," Willow laughed. "Like it's rolling across the land and going to chase us!"

"Or a flaming peach being hurled into the sky," said Uncle Delvan.

"Or one of the flaming marshmallows from the campfire," added Willow's dad with a chuckle.

Willow turned to Delia, expecting her to join in their silliness. But Delia looked as sad as she had back in the yard. Willow knew she was thinking about Aunt Deenie again.

"It will be all right," Willow whispered. "Don't let things bother you."

But Willow knew how much Delia worried. She draped her arm around her cousin's shoulder, and together they sat in the quiet stillness and watched another new day begin. Just as the last of the stars went out, Willow made another wish.

If only Uncle Delvan could find work.

If only Delia's mom and dad could be happy again.

If only . . .

Chapter 11
just peachy

An hour or so later they were back from the orchard, carrying bag after bag of fresh-picked peaches into the kitchen. The fathers poured themselves much-deserved cups of coffee and waited for directions from their daughters.

"What's next, Chef?" Willow's dad said. "Should I wash some peaches? Crack some eggs?"

"Sorry, Dad," Willow apologized, "but Delia and I are going to make the breakfast ourselves."

"You guys can cook together again when you get back to Chicago, Uncle Liam," promised Delia with a smile.

Uncle Delvan suggested the girls make peach pancakes. "Only if you want to. But I know those are your mom's favorite, Delia."

Delia seemed stunned that her dad still remembered something that made her mom happy. She stared speechlessly into his eyes, a few bright orange peaches thudding onto the floor. Willow bent down to retrieve them, telling Uncle Delvan that his idea was a good one.

"I've always dreamed of opening my own restaurant," Willow's dad said as he tucked a newspaper under his arm and headed for the porch chairs with Uncle Delvan. "I love the way food brings families together."

"Maybe I should consider cooking school, then," said Uncle Delvan, a hint of sadness in his voice. "We could use a little togetherness."

On their own in the kitchen now, the girls decided to cook up peach pancakes. Not only would those make Delia's mom happy, but they knew Aunt Rosie loved peaches, too. And they agreed that making breakfast would save Cat having to do it. Maybe that would repair the damage from the blueberry-smoothie disaster, not to mention Monday's lemonade incident.

Willow ran upstairs to get her notebook. She had clipped a pancake recipe from the newspaper last month and taped it to one of the pages. She was sure it was a winner.

"When do you think Cat starts cooking over here?" Willow asked, plopping her notebook onto the countertop and flipping through the pages. "I have no idea what time she shows up."

Delia said she'd noticed a few cars in Cat's driveway when she was carrying in the peaches. "Didn't Mr. Henry tell us real-estate people wanted her to sell the house? Maybe she's meeting with them right now."

They both agreed to get cooking, and fast.

First they washed the peaches. Then they mixed the flour and milk, paying close attention to their ingredients.

"Don't forget to throw in some vanilla," Willow added with a bounce. "It puts the cake in pancake!"

"Great," Delia replied. And dangling a ring of measuring spoons, she added, "But you can't just throw it in. You've got to measure things."

Willow rolled her eyes and took the spoons from Delia. She measured out one exact teaspoon of the vanilla, then dumped it into the bowl with a "Humph."

"Perfect." Delia smiled.

Before long, Cat appeared in the kitchen, looking red-faced and angry.

"What a morning," she growled, plunking down a basket that held only a few cucumbers and two small tomatoes. "It's bad enough that I have vultures circling my house. But now I have thieves stealing more of my vegetables. Someone is even taking my vegetable sauce right out of my pots! I tell you, if I catch that horse y'all call the family dog and that checker-playing rascal in my garden again, I'm gonna let them have it!"

Delia and Willow stood stunned at the stove. They blinked at Cat, too afraid to move even their spatulas. The only sound was the sizzling of warm peaches in the pan.

Now Willow knew why Mr. Henry had been sneaking around the garden by the tomato plants. They were Cat's vegetables!

"What are you two whippersnappers doing now?" Cat asked, her eyes quickly scanning the countertops for what might be broken, spilled, splattered, or otherwise wrecked.

Willow tried to speak, but her voice had deserted her. "Peach . . ." she squeaked.

". . . pancakes!" Delia finished.

Cat stared at them hard. Then she sniffed the air a few times. The aroma of warm peaches was mouth-watering. Willow slid her spatula under a pancake and flipped it. Delia was ready with a plate and fork.

"I can't resist cooked peaches," Cat confessed, her voice regaining some of its sunny Southern warmth. "How about I sit down right here and be your taste tester. Let's start with a stack of five of those flap-jacks. Give me your best shot."

And so the cousins did, mixing and pouring and flipping the peach pancakes as best they could. When they had five ready, Delia slid the plate across the island countertop and stared into Cat's face. Willow felt a bead of sweat trickle down her nose. The moment of truth was almost here.

Cat cleared her throat. She studied the pancake

stack from the left, then the right. She sniffed it, turned the plate, and sniffed again. Then she popped the lid off a bottle of maple syrup and poured it on.

"Did you use sugar or salt?" she demanded.

"Both," blurted the girls.

Cat nodded. Then she finally picked up her fork and cut into the stack. The world seemed to move in slow motion as she brought the triangle slice up to her lips. Delia's eyes were wide, and Willow could hear her cousin inhale. They grabbed each other's hands and watched every motion of Cat's jaw as she chewed.

"*Hooo-weee!*" Cat shouted after a few quiet moments.

Willow didn't know if that was good or bad. She and Delia pressed in closer, trying hard to read Cat's reaction.

"Girls," Cat finally said, licking a bit of syrup from her lips, "these flapjacks are delicious! I'm getting a taste of summertime with every bite."

"We were amazing," Willow announced a short while later, basking in a bit of pancake glory. She and Delia were climbing onto their boogie boards in the chilly water, not far from where Violet was swimming laps like she was at swim-team practice and Darlene was sunning herself on a bright purple beach towel. "Cat said they were the best she'd ever had."

"Not exactly," Delia corrected, diving into a wave, then coming up for air. "Cat said they were the best peach pancakes made by almost-ten-year-olds she'd ever had."

"I think it means we'll be baking cupcakes for this wedding, Delia. I just know it," she said, her boogie board running aground on the sandy beach. "Cat will help us cook, and Aunt Rosie will forget about those flower-girl dresses!"

Delia wasn't completely convinced. "My mom liked the pancakes, too," she reasoned, dragging her boogie board out of the water, "so that's two people who can tell Aunt Rosie how well we cook. But I think we need to do one more amazing thing, just to seal the deal."

And picking up her towel to dry off, Delia announced she was going to head back up to the kitchen and grab a stack of cookbooks for her and Willow to study. "Let's research the best possible thing to make for Aunt Rosie."

Willow dropped her board with a start. Study? Research? That sounded a bit like homework.

"Relax, Delia, we're on vacation," she said, pulling on her sun hat. "We can check the refrigerator later and come up with something to make. Plus I've got a whole notebook full of ideas we can throw together."

"Throw together?" said Delia, folding her arms and giving Willow a doubtful look.

"You've got to loosen up, Delia," Willow laughed. And flapping her arms, she added, "You know, like a loosey-goose!"

Just a little while later, as they climbed the steep bluff staircase back to the house, Willow heard a puffy bark coming from the far side of the yard. And immediately she knew that if Bernice was over there, then her little brother was, too.

"What is Sweet William doing now?" Delia asked.

She was pointing toward the edge of Cat's vegetable garden, where the showdown with Mother Goose had happened. "Is he dancing?"

"He's supposed to be playing checkers on the porch with Grandpa," Willow said with more than a little exasperation. "I hope he's not getting into trouble."

Both girls gazed over at Sweet William, tilting their heads first to one side, then to the other. Willow even tried squinting her eyes tight. No matter what she did, he still appeared to be waddling around like a duck. And Bernice was acting strangely too, scurrying to the left and right like she was dodging something.

"Now I see it," Delia laughed. And giving Willow's shoulder a playful nudge, she added, "It's exactly what you were talking about. There's your loosey-goose!"

And that's when Willow saw it, too.

"We've got a baby!" Sweet William was shouting, and he waved them over to see the broken goose egg. "And it thinks I'm its mama!"

Willow put her hands to her eyes, hoping the tiny yellow gosling would be gone when she opened them again. But it was still there.

"Delia, let's go to the kitchen," she moaned, leaning on her cousin's shoulder for support. "I'd rather spend the whole night studying cookbooks than deal with Sweet William and his new friend."

Delia and Willow's Taste-of-Summer Peach Pancakes

You can make the batter the night before, and the next morning wake up with only a little pouring and flipping left to do.

Ingredients:

2 cups flour

1 tablespoon baking powder

1 tablespoon sugar

1 teaspoon salt

2 cups milk

6 tablespoons butter, melted

2 eggs

1 teaspoon vanilla

2 large peaches, thinly sliced

Directions:

1. Make sure you have an adult's help.

2. Combine the flour, baking powder, sugar, and salt in a bowl. Be sure to measure and not just toss things in willy-nilly.

3. Add the milk, melted butter, eggs, and vanilla.

4. Whisk everything together, but don't overmix. It's okay to have a few lumps.

5. Heat a pan or griddle over medium-high heat and drop on a dab of butter.

6. Using a measuring cup, pour ¼ cup of pancake batter onto the hot pan. Really, you should measure this, too.

7. When you start to see bubbles, gently lay in some peach slices. Let the batter firm up slightly; then use a spatula to flip the pancakes. Cook another minute or so. Make sure your peaches smell warm and are sizzly, not burned.

8. Remove the pancakes to a large plate. Keep them warm by laying another plate or large bowl on top of them like a clamshell.

9. Serve with maple syrup. And wow your family and friends!

Makes about 12 pancakes.

Chapter 12
a periwinkle party

The next morning, Willow and Delia slipped on their flip-flops and headed downstairs to the kitchen, eager for their big chance to cook something amazing for Aunt Rosie. They were running out of time to convince her to put them in aprons instead of pink gowns.

"Today is Rosie's bridal shower," Delia reminded Willow. "If we can do something incredible in the kitchen now, she'll beg us to be her chefs!"

"Forget about sprinkling rose petals down the wedding aisle," Willow said as they hurried down the staircase. "She'll want us sprinkling chocolate toppings on all the desserts!"

Aunt Rosie was already in the dining room, arranging and rearranging the long table. She wore a bright blue sundress, and her thick brown hair was swept over one shoulder.

"You look beautiful in purply blue," Delia told her. And Willow agreed.

"Thank you, girls," Aunt Rosie said with a little curtsy. "It's periwinkle."

She was folding periwinkle-blue napkins, and periwinkle-blue place cards marked each seat at the table, which was draped in a periwinkle-blue cloth.

All that periwinkle was making Willow a little queasy.

"I want everything this exact shade of blue today," Aunt Rosie sighed. "It's the color of Jonathan's eyes, you know."

No, Willow thought, we didn't.

She glanced over at Delia, who raised a single eyebrow back. And in that moment, a silent pact passed between them, a pact so strong and obvious it needed no words. They would never, ever let themselves get so gaga over a boy that they matched their clothes and their parties to his eyeballs.

No way. Never. *Uh-uh.*

"Okay then," Delia sang in an overly merry voice, "we'll let you get back to work."

"Right," Willow agreed, "we're off to the kitchen to find Cat. Big day and all."

"Oh," Aunt Rosie said, her hands suddenly wringing a periwinkle napkin like it was a wet washcloth. "The kitchen? You're going to help Cat? Today?"

Willow thought she saw Aunt Rosie gulp. But Delia was poking Willow's shoulders and hurrying her along through the dining room, so she gave her aunt a friendly salute and dismissed the thought.

As they were about to push the door open into the kitchen, Grandma came marching out. Her floppy straw hat was poked through with tiny white flowers this morning, and she waved to them in her usual bright green gardening gloves.

"Girls, I bet you can't name three flowers that are blue," she began. "Rosie wants the whole house decorated in blue flowers, but I keep telling her that nature doesn't like blue. I've clipped blue cornflowers, but what else is there? There aren't even blue foods, for heaven's sake!"

The kitchen door swung open again, and Willow's dad and Uncle Delvan appeared behind Grandma, followed by Jonathan and his two brothers.

"She's right." Uncle Delvan grinned, giving Willow and Delia quick kisses on their foreheads. "There's rainbow trout, yellow perch, white bass. But nothing blue swimming out there in the lake."

Willow's dad said they were headed out for a day of fishing. "We'll try to catch something blue for Rosie."

"A fish to match Jonathan's eyes," teased Uncle

Delvan with a playful punch at Jonathan's shoulder. And the five fishermen said their farewells and tromped out the back door.

Delia reminded Grandma about blueberries. "There's one blue food."

"Yes, but beyond that? It's a challenge. Rosie always gives us a challenge!"

And Grandma pulled out her garden shears and headed for the front yard, setting off to snip more of Mr. Henry's flowers. But just before she left the dining room, she turned back to them with that suspicious look in her eyes again.

"Tomorrow is Rosie's wedding," she said, gesturing with the shears. "I expect you flower girls know how important today and tomorrow are to her."

"Of course we do," Delia said with a serious nod. And Willow got the feeling Grandma was calling them flower girls for a reason.

When they entered the kitchen, Cat was working quietly at the stove. Willow wasn't sure where they stood with her now. Yesterday's pancakes had been a delicious success. But the memories of the smoothies and the lemonade might still be fresh in Cat's mind.

Both girls looked around, eager to find something to do. Delia gathered dirty plates off the kitchen table and took them to the sink. Willow began pushing in stools around the island, eyeing the back wall for any smoothie spatter she might have missed.

"Back in Mississippi," Cat began softly, "I taught a cooking class. I was nicer then, could charm the fuzz off a peach. Well, I shared some of my secrets with my faithful students. I'll tell y'all right now, one of them is lemon zest. Lemons are the secret to the universe."

"I thought black holes were the secret to the universe," Delia said, forks clanging into the sink.

Cat laughed a big guffaw and scratched her head with the back of her hand, careful not to dirty her fingers. "Actually, it's black holes, lemons, and a stick of butter!"

She placed two large, white platters on the counter. When the girls stepped over to help, she didn't stop them. They arranged baby quiches made of spinach and bacon on one, and long bacon-wrapped asparagus spears on the other. Cat stood back when they were done, giving a quick nod of approval.

Willow's mind was racing. If they helped Cat with a few more tasks, maybe she would let them get cooking! She bounced a bit in her flip-flops. Any minute now, she might get to learn some tricks from a real chef. Willow could already imagine herself wearing one of those tall, white chef's hats.

Next up was a basket of tomatoes. Willow did the washing, Delia the drying. And Cat pulled out a sharp knife and began the slicing.

"What happened to that one?" Willow asked, pointing at what looked like a tomato crossed with an accordion. Its skin was ribbed like a pumpkin, but its coloring was fire-engine red.

"Those are fireworks for the mouth," came Mr. Henry's voice. He had just stepped into the kitchen and was tipping his straw sun hat to greet the three of them. "Ms. Catherine's heirloom tomatoes explode

with such flavor
and deliciousness,
you'll need a week to
recover."

Cat was actually batting her
eyelashes. She began to fan herself with
a small bunch of fresh-picked mint, telling Mr.
Henry to stop. But Willow didn't think she wanted
him to stop one bit. In fact, she thought Cat all of a
sudden looked a lot like Violet when she was talking
to a boy on the phone.

"The things Ms. Catherine coaxes from the dirt
out there," Mr. Henry said, nodding toward the

garden, "they're worthy of poetry. Dare I say, a symphony. She doesn't just have a green thumb; she has a golden one."

"Why, Mr. Henry," Cat stammered, all teasing gone from her face. "I never knew you felt that way about my tomatoes. I'm surprised—"

"There is a lot that might surprise you, Ms. Catherine," he said mysteriously. And again with a tip of his sun hat, Mr. Henry disappeared out the screen door. Willow thought she saw one of Cat's pots tucked under his arm, but she couldn't be sure.

Delia poured them each a glass of lemonade, freshly sweetened with what she promised was sugar. They all raised their glasses and clinked them together for a toast to Aunt Rosie's periwinkle party. Cat was clearly in a good mood after Mr. Henry's visit. She chattered on about tomatoes and gardening and getting her hands dirty.

"I'm crazy for bright red foods—tomatoes, raspberries, cherries. I'm like a hummingbird that way, going to all the bright red colors."

Willow and Delia told her about the hummingbirds they'd seen among the blueberry bushes. And Cat gave them a knowing grin.

"I'm so glad to hear y'all met my precious rubies," she said, slicing up more tomatoes. "I don't have diamonds; I don't have pearls. But I do have my ruby-throated hummingbirds. Can you believe those little beauties out there? They don't weigh more than a couple pennies. Yet they fly more than a thousand miles to come right back here to this spot, summer after summer."

Delia's face lit up when she heard this. "I believe it," she said, grinning.

"Me too," agreed Willow. "They're just like us!"

Chapter 13
hummingbirds and hungry bears

Cat let the cousins linger. But before Willow and Delia could even reach for a mixing bowl to start cooking, Cat packed them off with a plastic pitcher of sugar water and directions to refill the hummingbird feeders hanging on her property and around Whispering Pines.

"But we're here for the wedding shower," Delia began. "For Aunt Rosie!"

"We have to make something amazing," Willow pleaded, tossing out any idea she could think of. "A lemon tart or strawberry cupcakes. Maybe a blueberry cheesecake!"

Delia jabbed Willow with her elbow.

"Forget about blueberries," Willow squeaked, not wanting to bring up unpleasant smoothie memories. "We can make something periwinkle!"

Cat shook her head, telling them she was too busy for any more talking. And before they knew it, Willow and Delia were stepping off the back porch and into the bright morning with clear marching orders.

"Just be mindful of the creakers over there," she called after them. "I've got a few creaky old steps, inside and out. If you're not careful, that old house will eat you right up."

Willow and Delia grudgingly said good-bye and headed for the wooden gate.

"*Uh-oh,*" Delia said, coming to a halt. "Should we bring Sweet William?"

Both girls looked around until they caught sight of Sweet William near the front of the house. He was playing leapfrog with Jonathan and his brothers on the lawn while Bernice supervised nearby. There were fishing poles propped up along the porch, and

Willow could see her dad loading things into the back of their car.

Delia pointed out the red pail on the porch steps, and they figured frogs were inside. Or perhaps the gosling, which Sweet William had begun calling Gossie.

"He looks occupied for now," Willow said. "Come on, let's go."

They walked along the white fence until they reached the arched gate. Delia carried Cat's pitcher gingerly, trying not to spill the syrupy water. Willow snapped off a handful of honeysuckle and buried her nose in its sweet fragrance as they walked.

She looked past the faded ART GALLERY sign and across the long yard toward the blueberry bushes, hoping to glimpse one of the hummingbirds. Between the rubies, the wheat penny, and wishing on stars each night, the cousins had good luck to spare.

"I wonder when we're really going to feel all this luck," she began. Then, bumping Delia's shoulder in excitement, she said, "Maybe we'll find a treasure chest on the beach. Or get free ice-cream sundaes at Blue Moo Creamery."

"Maybe all the good luck is piling up for the wedding tomorrow," Delia said, a little more sugar water sloshing out of the pitcher, "and we won't have to be flower girls after all."

Once the girls reached the old yellow house, they found two feeders hanging on the back porch. They climbed the creaky stairs, careful not to fall through one of the steps where the wood was badly rotted. Willow dragged a rickety chair over to the first feeder and held it steady while Delia climbed on.

Just as they finished pouring Cat's nectar into the second one, Willow heard a fierce growling that nearly stopped her heart. She stumbled back into Delia's chair, nearly knocking her cousin to the ground.

"What was that?" Willow gasped. "A bobcat? A badger?"

"Those are both possibilities in Michigan," Delia reasoned calmly. Then in a tiny voice, she whispered, "But it could also be a bear."

"A bear? Do something, Delia! You went to zoo camp!"

"At zoo camp," she gulped, "the animals were in cages!"

Growwwwl.

Bark.

"Sweet William? Is that you?"

Around the side of the house came a hand and then a scrunched-up face, which was pretty ferocious for a kindergartner.

Bernice appeared behind Sweet William, looking delighted at their trick. She barked an enthusiastic greeting and wagged her bandaged tail. Not far behind them waddled a noisy, peeping Gossie.

"What are you guys doing?" Sweet William asked, squeezing his skinny body through the wooden slats and onto the porch. "I thought you were going to play with me."

"You're right, we were," Willow said, dragging the chair back to its proper place. "I mean, we are. But no more trying to scare us, okay?"

Sweet William nodded and pressed his face against a dusty window to peer into the old house. He sounded surprised when Delia told him Cat lived here. Or maybe "lived" was an exaggeration. She seemed to sleep over here but spend the rest of her time working at Whispering Pines.

"I thought this was a forest house for the animals, like chipmunks and squirrels and deer," Sweet William said.

"It's no wonder Cat doesn't want to be over here," Willow said, brushing a cobweb from her hair. "The place looks like it hasn't been lived in for a hundred years."

Sweet William pointed at a row of paintings leaning against the far wall. "I like Uncle Delvan's pictures better than those."

When Delia heard that, she stopped scratching Bernice's ears and scrambled to her feet. Cupping her hands around her eyes, she also peeked through the window. Together they counted fifteen paintings propped up along the length of the main room.

"This old place must have been an art gallery once," Delia whispered. "Just like that sign says, out by the big tree in the yard."

Willow looked over at Delia, and she could practically see the wheels turning in her cousin's mind.

"Cat should clean this place up," Delia was saying to herself. "She could hang these old paintings back on the walls, give the house a fresh coat of paint . . ."

Even though the cobwebs and dusty windows made it hard to see, one thing was perfectly clear to Willow. Delia Dees had an idea.

Chapter 14
helping hands, paws, and jaws

Thwack!
Thwack!
Thwack!

The screen door announced the three cousins' return to the kitchen. But Willow remembered that they should keep Bernice far away from Cat.

Thwack! again.

She ushered Bernice and Sweet William back out onto the porch, promising fresh lemonade and a few treats if he'd sit still for a while and play with his modeling clay. Grandpa was at the far end of the porch in his favorite chair, reading the newspaper.

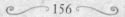

"How are we this fine morning, my grandchildren?" he asked, setting his paper on his lap and rocking back and forth. "Have you been off exploring the wonders of the great outdoors?"

"We were next door at that old house," Delia replied, walking down to greet him. "It's kind of creepy and overgrown with weeds over there. But with a little help, it could be nice instead of scary."

Grandpa nodded and gazed out at the Sutherland yard.

"What are the scariest flowers in the garden?" he asked them. And rocking a few beats in his chair, he answered, "The tiger lily and the snapdragon!"

Sweet William hooted and slapped his knee. And Willow chuckled as she crossed the porch and gave Grandpa a peck on the cheek. She made sure to block his view of Gossie, who was waddling under the porch with Bernice to take a nap. Then she helped Sweet William arrange the figures he'd sculpted and the colorful hunks of unmolded clay.

"I picked up some acorns and sticks when we were at the old yellow house," Sweet William said, emptying his pockets onto the porch table. "I think I'll make some Twig People. They can be friends with the Clay Family."

With Sweet William and the animals taken care of, the girls slipped back into the kitchen. Willow popped her head into the dining room. Aunt Rosie was still fussing over the periwinkle-blue table, making sure everything was just so. Willow's mom and Aunt Deenie were buzzing around Rosie like honeybees in a garden of blue. Violet and Darlene were busy in the front hall, helping Grandma arrange blue flowers—Willow thought they were called hydrangeas—in a row of tall vases.

Cat was nowhere in sight. But in the kitchen, every inch of counter space was filled with cake plates, platters, and serving trays holding the most amazing treats: the quiches and asparagus, perfectly square finger sandwiches, beautifully arranged fruits and cheeses. Some of the food was for today's shower, but Cat was getting most of it ready for tomorrow's wedding.

One fancy plate held a fruit tart that looked so flawless that Willow had to touch it to make sure the strawberries, kiwis, and blueberries weren't made of plastic.

"Cat hasn't left us much to do," Delia said, trying to find room at the overflowing sink to wash her hands. "We could serve the Good & Plenty and the Mentos. But that's not so impressive."

Willow agreed. They needed to do something really big to get Rosie's attention. But what?

"I'm covered in sticky hummingbird nectar," Delia complained, heading for the upstairs bathroom. "I need to wash this off before the mosquitoes eat me."

Willow asked her to grab the polka-dotted bag and bring it with her when she came back downstairs.

"It's got my recipe notebook. There's got to be something in there that can help us today."

Willow poured two lemonades to take out to her brother and Grandpa. But the kitchen was quiet now, and she couldn't help overhearing snippets of conversation coming from the dining room. Still holding the jug of lemonade, she stepped closer toward the swinging door and pushed it open just a crack, letting the voices slip in.

"I love being a nurse," Aunt Deenie was saying, "but I can't keep working so many shifts. It's killing me. Sure, it pays the bills. But there's no time to talk anymore. . . ."

Willow knew eavesdropping was wrong—Delia would never do it in a million years. But she had to find out what was happening to her aunt and uncle.

"Maybe Delvan is lost right now," Aunt Rosie said. "Our jobs define us. They tell the rest of the world who we are. What does it say when you don't have a job?"

Willow heard a noise behind her and nearly

jumped out of her flip-flops. She whipped around and found Sweet William standing there, sipping the lemonade she'd poured. Bernice stood beside him, one furry ear raised as if asking Willow what she was up to.

"Oh, it's just you guys," Willow sighed, setting the jug of lemonade onto the counter. "That other glass is for Grandpa, if you don't mind taking it out to him."

"Sure," Sweet William said. "Grandpa, Bernice, and me were just talking about how it was time for a snack."

Willow turned back to the dining-room door and silently inched it open again. She didn't want to miss a word.

". . . he's a talented engineer . . . so creative . . ." her mom was saying. "It's just a matter of time, but he will find work again."

"That's the thing," Aunt Deenie said, her voice tight with worry. "This experience has made him think about what he wants out of life. And working for a big company isn't it. Delvan wants something else."

"Like what?" Aunt Rosie asked.

"I don't know," Aunt Deenie said. "He's still searching."

Suddenly a face appeared at the heavy door, and Willow found herself nose-to-nose with Violet. Willow jumped back as her big sister pushed into the kitchen and eyed her suspiciously.

"I don't know what you're up to in here, Willow. But it's time for you to clear out. Darlene and I are taking over."

Willow was confused. What did Violet mean by *taking over*? Her sister didn't know the first thing about cooking. Violet had a long list of things she was great at, but operating an oven was not one of them.

"Darlene ran upstairs to get T-shirts for us to throw on so we don't dirty our dresses," Violet explained, adjusting the straps of her bright orange sundress. "We're going to whip up some cupcakes for Aunt Rosie's shower. Now scoot, go, shoo."

Willow bristled. Not only was it insulting that Violet assumed she could cook, but it was doubly insulting that Violet thought she could just shoo Willow away like she was a wayward pigeon. This space belonged to her and to Delia. Not to mention Cat.

"No way. Never. *Uh-uh*," Willow said, trying to keep her voice calm and steady the way Delia always did. "Cupcakes are my thing, Violet. Not yours."

Violet threw her head back and laughed. But when she saw Willow's seriousness, she stopped.

"I mean it, Violet. Delia and I are planning something in here. Just leave us alone, all right?"

"If you're still trying to get out of wearing those flower-girl dresses, you two need to give it up already," Violet moaned, stepping aside to let Sweet William scoot past. "You're not going to convince Aunt Rosie to let you off."

Willow fidgeted with a spoon on the countertop and took a deep breath. Violet used to be fun, and Darlene, too. It was only last summer that they'd organized a talent show on the back porch for the whole family. But this summer they were different. It was like they spoke a different language from Willow and Delia.

"It's not only about those pink dresses anymore," Willow began. "It's about Cat, too. She's really good at cooking. She can teach me things."

"You aren't serious about being a chef, are you?" Violet scoffed.

Willow stared down at the spoon in silence. She wasn't about to admit that to Violet. If she did, she'd never hear the end of her teasing.

"Cat doesn't have time to mess around with you, Willow. She's got problems up to her earlobes. But

you might not have noticed since you're so obsessed with the pink dresses."

Willow felt her hands ball up into fists. She wanted to shout at Violet that she did know about Cat's problems, and that she really wanted to do something about them.

"Violet, Cat can help me learn some things about cooking," Willow said, using all the patience she could possibly muster. "And, well . . . Delia and I can help her, too. We know how! So let us do that, okay? Please?"

Just then Delia appeared, with Darlene right on her heels.

"Did you hear this?" Delia asked, her voice practically hissing as she dropped Willow's polka-dotted bag on the kitchen floor with a loud thud. "Darlene says they're going to make cupcakes. Cupcakes! *Cup. Cakes.*"

Willow shot a pleading look at Violet, her eyes doing all the talking now. Her sister had to understand how much this meant to her.

"Never mind, Darlene," Violet finally said. And she took the T-shirts from Darlene's arms and shoved them onto a kitchen stool. "Let's go pick some mint leaves. Aunt Rosie said she wants to serve peppermint iced tea to all her shower guests."

And to Willow and Delia's great relief, their sisters pushed through the swinging door and back into the dining room, leaving them all alone.

Well, almost alone.

Willow heard it first. But Delia was quicker to spin around and face the calamity behind them.

It was big and furry. And it was chewing.

"Bernice!" they shrieked together. "Nooooo!"

Bernice's jaws were just finishing off Cat's bacon quiches. And the platter of bacon-wrapped asparagus was already licked clean.

When Bernice heard the girls, she obediently sat down. But it was too late. Sweet William turned his face up to look at Delia and Willow panting over his head. Crumbs clung to his lips, and a half-eaten slice of fruit tart rested in his fingers. Willow saw he'd already cut a second slice, probably to share with Grandpa over a checkers match.

What were they going to do?

Thwack!

All three heads turned (plus a fourth, furry one) at the sound of the screen door. And Willow knew who was standing there before her eyes even landed on that angry face.

Cat plunked down a basket filled with long loaves of bread. And with one glance around the kitchen, she took in the latest disaster.

"I hope y'all brought shovels," she snarled, "because you're in a heaping pile of trouble."

Quick & Easy
If-You're-Ever-in-a-Jam Mini Quiches

Ingredients:

1 frozen pastry sheet, thawed and unrolled

2 slices deli ham, cut into small chunks

½ cup spinach leaves, sliced

1 cup shredded cheese, such as cheddar, Monterey Jack, or Colby

1 cup milk

5 eggs

1 teaspoon salt

1 pinch black pepper

¼ teaspoon nutmeg

Directions:

1. Make sure you have an adult's help.

2. Heat oven to 375 degrees, then grease a 12-cup muffin tin.

3. Once the pie pastry has thawed from the freezer, lay it onto wax paper. Using the top of a drinking glass, cut 12 dough circles from the pie pastry. Lay the circles in the greased muffin-tin cups, stretching and tucking them into place.

4. Drop whatever toppings you like in each cup. We suggest ham chunks, spinach, and shredded cheese. You can choose any cheese you like or mix up your favorites. Distribute the toppings evenly among all the muffin cups. You can use other foods, like green onions or red bell peppers, too.

5. In a medium bowl, combine the milk, eggs, salt, pepper, and nutmeg. Then spoon the mixture evenly into each of the 12 muffin-tin cups using a ¼-cup measuring cup.

6. Bake 20 minutes, or until a toothpick inserted into the center of a quiche comes out clean.

Makes 12 mini quiches.

Chapter 15

boogie boards, sand castles, and summer secrets

It was a few hours later, though it felt to Willow like an eternity, when they were able to escape the kitchen cleanup and Cat's anger and finally disappear. She'd made them scrub the plates Bernice had licked and wrap more asparagus stalks with bacon. Both girls could have cried for joy when they saw Cat pull a container of extra mini quiches out of the refrigerator—all hope was not lost. But the fruit tart brought real tears to their eyes.

Cat had to make an entirely new one from scratch.

Just as she pulled the shell from the oven, Cat stiffly asked them to leave. Willow and Delia couldn't get out of the kitchen fast enough. They'd run out of ways to say they were sorry.

Neither cousin knew what to do with all their nervous energy, so they decided a long walk on the beach might be best. It would let them clear their minds and their guilty consciences.

"I haven't seen your wheat penny in a while," Delia said as they crossed the dunes and made their way toward the lighthouse. "Do you know where it is?"

Willow tugged her sun hat on, then rummaged around in her pockets. "It must be in my other shorts. Maybe lucky pennies only work if you carry them with you."

Skirting the edge of the water, wet sand squishing under their feet, the cousins walked beside the big blue lake and wondered about their luck. How could it be this bad when they had so many things on their side? Were hummingbirds only lucky the moment you saw them? Did wishing on stars only work when you were directly beneath them?

A good while later, as they made their way back

from the lighthouse, Willow and Delia were still not ready to head back up the stairs. They saw Grandpa stretched out on the beach in a lounge chair, reading a magazine. Sweet William was nearby, building a sand castle beside the big rainbow-patterned beach umbrella.

The girls decided Grandpa and Sweet William looked like better company than what was waiting at the top of the bluff.

Delia plopped down on a purple towel, probably left behind by Darlene. Willow sat on another one under the umbrella, scooting into the shade. She didn't want to get any more freckles than necessary this summer.

Sweet William watched them for a few moments, then scratched his cheek with a sandy finger and apologized for eating Cat's food.

"I'm sorry if me and Bernice messed up Aunt Rosie's shouter," he said sadly.

"I think you mean shower," Delia corrected with a sigh.

"But it was a shouter. The yellow-haired lady in the kitchen was shouting like crazy."

"No, Sweet William, that food was for tomorrow's wedding and today's *shower*," Willow explained, trying hard to keep her patience. "It's a party where people give the bride presents."

"Shower? Well, Aunt Rosie seems clean enough to me," he said, turning his attention back to his sand castle. "I wouldn't give her a bath, either."

Bernice let out a gentle bark and wagged her tail as if she were apologizing along with Sweet William. She was sprawled in the shade underneath a picnic table, hiding from the August sun just like Willow. Gossie was snuggled into a shallow hole beside the castle moat.

Grandpa tipped up the brim of his sun hat and waved to the girls. Then he went back to his magazine.

"I don't think Grandpa and Grandma have noticed yet," Delia said, eyeing the tiny yellow goose.

"You're right," Willow agreed. "Gossie is our summer secret."

Despite all the evidence a gosling left behind.

"I know another summer secret," Delia said, rolling onto her side and letting a ladybug crawl up her arm. "Mr. Henry is up to something."

"That's just what I think!" said Willow, flopping onto her stomach and listing all the possibilities for Mr. Henry. "He could be a spy. He could be a secret agent . . ."

Delia said she thought Mr. Henry was teaching himself how to cook. "But I don't exactly know why he's so sneaky about it. I thought I saw him carry off a whole pot of Cat's vegetable sauce."

"Me too," said Willow. "Maybe he's embarrassed that he's not as good a cook as we are. Next time we get in the kitchen, we should teach him a few things."

Delia said she didn't know if there would be another next time. Cat was really angry.

Willow was quiet for a few moments. She watched the ladybug stretch its wings on Delia's arm.

"I haven't told anyone this, Delia, but . . ." And she paused, losing her courage.

"But what?"

"But"—and Willow took a deep breath—"I really want to cook with Cat. To learn from her. Because someday I want . . ." And she let her voice trail off again.

"You want to be a professional chef? I already know that about you, Willow," Delia said, grinning. "You'll make a great one."

Willow smiled back at her cousin. She didn't have to worry about Delia making fun of her idea or telling her she wasn't any good. And she didn't even have to wonder how Delia already knew. It was their amber eyes. They really did see things the same way.

The ladybug fluttered its wings, then flew away in the breeze. The girls sat quietly, watching the water. A few seagulls bobbed in the waves.

"If Cat would just let us back into her kitchen," Delia said, digging her toes deeper into the sand, "she could show us her cooking secrets. But even more important, we could help her with all that catering. She could have a good business someday, if she just had a little help."

Willow scrambled to her knees and pulled off her sun hat, stretching across the sand to look right into her cousin's eyes. Delia's pupils were inches from her own, their noses nearly touching.

"What in the world are you doing?" laughed Delia.

"Seeing eye to eye." Willow grinned, blinking a few times. Then she plopped back under the umbrella. "Because I was thinking the exact same thing as you. Since we've gotten to know about Cat and what's happening next door . . . well, it feels different. Suddenly it's not so important to impress Aunt Rosie. It's more important to help Cat with her catering business."

Bernice slipped out from beneath the picnic table and came over to the two cousins, her tail wagging happily. She circled them a few times, then lay down in Willow's patch of shade. Delia hopped up and moved one of the sand buckets closer to Sweet William's moat, making sure to block any chance of Grandpa catching sight of Gossie.

"Since we've got a few summer secrets now," Delia

whispered, "I'll tell you mine. But you have to promise to keep it that—a secret."

Willow pretended to zip her lips.

Delia scooted her towel closer toward Willow and Bernice and the umbrella. She began talking about the Sutherland house and how it could be an art gallery, like it once was.

"Here's my idea," she said a little breathlessly. "I think Cat could sell her food there. You know, make it a gallery and café."

Willow said she loved the idea. But Delia wasn't through.

"We just need to help rebuild the place. It would take carpenters, construction people. But we have a big family. We could all lend a hand. Because if Cat doesn't do something soon, she's going to lose her house."

Willow couldn't speak for a moment. Her thoughts were doing somersaults in her head. Delia was worried about Cat losing her home. But what about Delia's house back in Detroit? From what Willow's parents were whispering, if Uncle Delvan didn't find work soon, the Dees family might lose their house, too.

Willow stared at her cousin, searching for a word. Delia was the exact opposite of selfish. But what was it? *Other*ish? Sel*fless*?

Then a thought struck.

"Delia, you're onto something. What if we did help Cat fix up her house and turn it into an art gallery and café? And then"—she paused, surprised by her own emotions—"what if your dad sold his paintings there?"

Delia's eyes grew big, and she didn't speak for a few moments. Clambering over from her beach towel to Willow's, she slipped into the tiny patch of shade beside Bernice. Delia was so flustered, she hugged Bernice around the neck and tried to give Willow's knees a friendly scratching. Then she caught herself, and gave Bernice a good scratch and threw her arms around Willow's neck.

For the next long while—Willow wasn't sure how long it was—they talked about the possibilities for

Cat, for Uncle Delvan, and for the whole family. Like waves washing on the beach, their ideas came one after the other. Just talking about the old Sutherland house, even if nothing ever came of their ideas, made them both feel good.

Chapter 16
mr. henry's shed

*L*ater that afternoon, Willow and Delia crossed the busy yard, past crews getting ready for Rosie's wedding, to Mr. Henry's shed. They wanted to find out about his summer secret. And they decided to let him in on one of theirs.

Even though he wasn't technically a Bumpus, Mr. Henry felt like family. Not only did the girls trust his opinion, but they both agreed that if anyone could pitch their idea to their parents, he would be the perfect person. It wouldn't sound so far-fetched coming from an adult, especially when the adult was Mr. Henry.

So as they got to talking, he sat on a bench in his shed and nodded, offering them the occasional "umm-hmm" as he listened to their plans for the old Sutherland house.

"And not only could we sell my dad's paintings at the art gallery," Delia exclaimed, "but we could get Cat to sell her food there, too!"

"An art gallery and café!" shouted Willow, loving the idea as it grew bigger and bigger. "We can call it Paintings and Pastries! Or Arts and Eats! Or maybe the Great Gulps Gallery and Café! People will go crazy for Cat's food. And you even said it the other night when we were roasting marshmallows: Cat needs to reach more people than she does cooking here at Whispering Pines."

Both girls were jumping up and down now, causing a minor earthquake in Mr. Henry's hobby shed. Until the sound of rattling glasses made them both stop.

"What's that noise?" asked Delia, peering around at the cluttered shelves.

"That's a little something I've been working on," Mr. Henry answered, placing his sun hat on a nearby worktable and pulling a canning jar off a shelf. "And as with your idea, it relates to Ms. Catherine and her culinary career. Have you ever had the pleasure of tasting her vegetable sauce?"

And now it was Mr. Henry's turn to talk.

The cousins sat listening, side by side on a narrow wooden bench across from him. As he spoke, Willow nudged Delia with her shoulder, barely able to contain her excitement. And Delia nudged her right back.

Because it was one thing to be in on a secret, but it was another thing entirely to be in on a delicious one.

They were back down on the beach with Grandpa when the girls heard the call that pizza was being served.

"We're having pizza now?" asked Sweet William, puzzled why they were eating lunch so late in the day. Or was it that they were having dinner so early?

"Let's call it *linner*," said Willow, who was stowing their boogie boards under the picnic table where Bernice had been napping.

"Or *dunch*," offered Delia, waving good-bye to Grandpa as he headed up the stairs.

"Mom wants us to go to bed early since Aunt

Rosie's wedding is tomorrow morning," Willow explained. "So she's moved up our dinnertime."

Sweet William watched Gossie poke around in the sand.

"Can we have a morning avenger together tomorrow," Sweet William asked, "just like you had with Dad and Uncle Delvan?"

"I think you mean *adventure*," corrected Delia.

"Peach picking, you mean?" asked Willow, sitting down on the sand next to her little brother.

"Right," he said, clasping his hands together like he was begging. "It's been almost a whole week, and we haven't done anything fun."

"We've taken you boogie boarding," Willow pointed out. "Wasn't that fun?"

"Fun enough," he answered with a dejected shrug. "But it's not an avenger—I mean adventure. I want to do something exciting with you."

185

Delia ran her hand through Sweet William's curls. "Sorry, little cousin, but we can't have any adventures tomorrow. It's too important for Aunt Rosie that we're ready for her wedding."

And that meant putting on those awful pink dresses. Willow tossed a skipping stone onto the beach and stared off toward the water. It was too late—too late to impress Aunt Rosie with their cooking skills, too late to get out of the flower-girl jobs. But worst of all, it was too late with Cat. They'd made her so angry that there was no chance she'd ever let them help her make the food for the wedding reception.

Turning away from the water, Willow stared up at Whispering Pines and at the overgrown Sutherland place next door. How could it be Friday evening already? When the week began, all she and Delia could think about was cooking their way out of the flower-girl jobs. But now they had bigger things on their minds than having to wear pink dresses.

And there was no time left to make things right.

Sweet William started to beg again, but Delia had already gathered up her belongings and begun the long climb up the stairs to pizza. Willow picked up her sunblock and blue hat and trudged through the sand right behind her.

But just as she passed Darlene's and Violet's purple towels, something shiny caught her eye: Violet's gold medals from her swim meets. Willow stopped short. Should she leave them there, even kick a bit more sand over them so she'd never have to see them again? Willow was tempted.

Once they reached the top of the bluff, Violet and Darlene were waiting. Darlene stood there with her arms folded across her chest, looking down over her sunglasses at them. Violet was clutching their flowery bouquets from the wedding rehearsal and looking like an angry pom-pom girl. She was scowling at Bernice and Gossie.

"Willow," Violet warned with a huffy breath, "you have got to get rid of that duck."

"Duck?"

"Goose," corrected Delia.

"That's my favorite game!" cheered Sweet William. "Can we play it now?"

Violet passed the honey-suckle bouquets to Darlene and hotly explained to her brother that they weren't playing any games. Then, turning to Willow, she began flailing her arms this way and that as she fired off a list of complaints.

"How could you let him find another pet? Have you seen his collection of frogs? He's got them in the bathtub up on the third floor. They're green and gross and covered in disgusting brown spots."

Willow tried to imagine being a crossing guard just like Delia and keeping her voice calm. But it was no use.

"Well, why weren't you looking after Sweet William when you're the oldest"—not to mention bossiest know-it-all, she wanted to add—"kid in the family?"

Darlene said they had been busy with wedding preparations. "It's not easy being junior bridesmaids," she explained, trying to look older than her twelve years. "There are a lot of responsibilities."

"But you guys wouldn't know about that," added Violet, whose expression made Willow want to squirt her with the bottle of sunblock in her hand. "You've been too busy trying to make Cat look bad."

"That's not true at all," Willow protested.

"We're trying to help her, not hurt her," Delia said firmly.

Willow couldn't believe her ears. Was that how it looked? When everything they'd done this week was either to impress Aunt Rosie or to win over Cat? They hadn't been trying to make a mess of things. But somehow that was how it had turned out.

Willow felt a sinking feeling in her stomach. She squeezed her eyes shut, but all she could see was blue, which made her think of Aunt Rosie's periwinkle party they'd skipped out on. The whole week was feeling like one giant disaster.

She fumbled with her sun hat, pulling out the gold medals from the beach and pressing them toward her sister.

"Here, take these," Willow said gruffly. "It'd be such a shame if you lost them. What would we do without your medals to remind everybody which Sweeney sister is the talented one and which is the one who always messes up?"

Violet went stiff, the gold glinting in her hands. She shook her head as if to say it wasn't true, but Willow looked away.

"You two need to go make nice with Cat," Darlene said, tugging the sunblock from Willow's hands and shoving the two bouquets of honeysuckle, daisies, and zinnias in its place. "She's reached Bumpus Family Overload and is threatening to quit."

"Flowers always help," Violet said, trying to catch Willow's eye. "Tell her you're sorry, that it won't happen again, and you'll keep a close watch on Sweet

William and Bernice and her garden. Maybe that will make things better."

Willow and Delia made the long march down the path to the kitchen steps, Violet's and Darlene's bouquets in hand. When they reached the screen door, they saw Cat inside, sitting on a stool at the center island and slicing a slab of bacon. She was mumbling to herself and chopping with what Willow thought was a little too much enthusiasm.

The girls knocked on the screen door, then let themselves in with heads hung low. Cat told them the pizza was next door, over at her property.

"Breakfast will be there tomorrow, too," she said tightly. "The Whispering Pines kitchen is officially closed for business."

Had Cat really quit?

Willow and Delia started speaking at the same time, apologizing for the salty lemonade, the spattered smoothies, Sweet William's cucumber swords, and Bernice's bacon obsession. And they told her how excited they were to taste what she was serving at tomorrow's reception, how much they still wanted to help out, and how much they believed in her cooking.

"I just sold my cow, y'all," Cat interrupted flatly, "so you can keep your bull."

Willow wanted to run right out of the room. How would they ever get Cat to forgive them? But Delia straightened her shoulders, thrust her and Willow's hands forward, and awkwardly presented Cat with their bouquets.

"We brought you these," she said, her crossing-guard voice clear and steady. "A peace offering. We know how important tomorrow is to you. And we want to help you get ready for it."

Willow wanted to do something, too—anything! So she picked up a pitcher sitting on the counter nearby and shoved the bouquets inside. She filled it with water, nervously arranged the flowers, and held it up for Cat to smell.

"These are from all of us—the whole family," she announced, pushing the honeysuckle closer to Cat's

nose. "We're all behind you. So please don't quit."

Cat stared at the flowers, her eyes nearly crossing. Then, finally, she cleared her throat.

"I appreciate you coming in here to talk to me," she began, firmly pushing the pitcher back toward Willow. "And I apologize for getting upset. But you've done just about enough for one week. So if y'all don't mind heading over for your pizza, I'll get down to business. Just mind the creakers over there. I've got porch steps and inside steps that need to be fixed in that old house."

Willow and Delia begged for even just the

teensiest task to help her. Looking around at the pots on the stove and platters on the countertops, it was clear there was still work to be done.

"Can't we do something?" Delia offered.

"Anything?" Willow added.

"There is one thing," Cat said with a sneeze. "Could one of you—*achoo!*—bring me—*achoo!*—my allergy medicine?"

Delia dashed over to the cabinet by the sink and pulled out an amber container with a round white lid. By the time she returned, Cat's eyes were red and watery as if she'd been crying.

"I've always," she explained through a few more fits of sneezing, "been allergic to honeysuckle." Then, as if to drive that point home, she sneezed the loudest sneeze Willow had ever heard: *"Ahh-CHOO!"*

Willow quickly moved the pitcher of flowers aside. Then she set a water glass down on Cat's cutting board, which was covered with bacon and strange fruits that looked a lot like brown plums. Cat popped the medicine into her mouth, then gulped down the entire glass of water. She handed it back to Willow to refill.

"I've been working on the finger foods. Y'all better keep that dog away from these bacon-wrapped dates," Cat said a few moments later, dabbing a tissue to her eyes and sniffling. Finally, she relented just a little. "I guess you girls can help me pull out the cakes."

Cat opened the refrigerator and grabbed two bowls full of frosting, one pink and the other white. She set them on the counter with a *clunk, clunk*. Then she let out a few more sneezes. Delia and Willow stepped over to the refrigerator and pulled out two circular layers of the wedding cake, while Cat went back for the next two.

"Four tiers of love, lots and lots of pink. That's what your aunt Rosie asked for, and that's what I aim to give her," Cat said, her eyes scanning the whole kitchen now and all the work she had yet to finish. Finally, her gaze came back to rest on Delia and Willow and their pleading faces.

"We're actually pretty amazing bakers," Delia began. "Willow can crack open eggs one-handed!"

"Just give us one more chance," Willow begged.

Cat blew her nose into a hankie, then took a long drink of water and washed her hands at the sink. She picked up her knife again and started slicing more bacon.

"I guess y'all can come by here in the morning. I might let you make the lemonade—that's something I know you'll get right this time. But now you two need to skedaddle. I'm going to be busy as a moth in a mitten tonight."

Couldn't-Be-Easier-Unless-There's-a-Dog-Around Appetizers

Ingredients:

4 pieces uncooked bacon

12 pitted dates

Directions:

1. Make sure you have an adult's help.

2. Make sure your dog cannot get into the kitchen.

3. Move oven rack to top third of oven. Heat oven to 425 degrees. Stack the bacon together and slice into thirds, making sure the three sections are of even lengths.

4. Wrap each bacon section around a date and secure with a toothpick. If the dates are not pitted, just cut a slit down one side and pull out the seed. Make sure to poke the toothpick through both sides of the bacon and date.

5. Lay each bacon-wrapped date on a baking sheet covered with parchment paper.

6. Bake for 4 minutes. Flip, and bake on other side another 4 minutes.

7. Let cool completely and enjoy with your family, friends, or dog.

Makes 12 bacon-wrapped dates.

Chapter 18
wedding day,
very, very early

Willow heard the alarm go off, and she pulled the pillow over her head. The room was still dark, like it had been on the morning of their sunrise adventure.

"Get up," Delia said, poking Willow in the legs and sides. "Cat said we could come down and help with the wedding. This is our big chance to do something in her kitchen."

Willow slid farther under the covers, pulling the pillow with her.

"Cat said we could help with the lemonade, Delia. We're not going to learn to be world-class chefs making lemonade. So what's the point?"

Delia tugged the covers off and tried to drag her floppy cousin out of bed.

"Let's get dressed and get down there! We can start with the lemonade, and after that Cat will give us more. We can be her catering team if we hurry up!"

Willow dove back onto her squeaky bed and clamped the pillow over her head.

"What's the rush? The wedding is at eleven o'clock, and it takes about five minutes to make lemonade. After that, Cat's just going to kick us out of the kitchen. So I'm going back to sleep."

But Delia would not be put off. Willow heard her thumping around the room. Then she felt something hit her shoulder.

"There are your shoes for the wedding," Delia said, just as a second object smacked Willow on the rump. "And you better sit up, because I'm about to throw your gown."

Willow popped up just in time to catch the puffy pink ball. It was no use fighting her cousin—in fact, it was no use trying to fight the flower-girl dresses anymore. It was just another item to add to her long list of things that didn't go right this week.

"We got away with not having our baskets at the rehearsal," Willow sighed, finally putting her bare feet on the wood floor. "But I don't think we can get away with not having our dresses today. Right?"

They both went silent as the idea of hiding their gowns hung in the air.

"I think we both love Aunt Rosie too much to do that to her," Delia said, tugging her own gown off its hanger. "She wants this day to be perfect."

"You're right," Willow agreed, coming back to her senses. "I'd hate to see Aunt Rosie disappointed. This is supposed to be the most special day of her life."

Both girls dressed in silence, barely able to look at each other. Willow knew that no matter how awful Delia looked in her gown, she herself probably looked ten times worse.

Was this how pirates felt before they had to walk the plank?

They took turns zipping each other up and tying the enormous pink sashes in back. And since their moms had made them wash their hair last night before bed, Willow's curls were a tangled mess. Delia helped calm them down, pulling Willow's hair back in a white headband and letting the long spirals do their own thing.

They both agreed: *no buns.*

Willow smoothed Delia's hair into her usual

perfect braids, tying white ponytail holders to the ends. Then she slid a matching white headband into her cousin's hair.

They both decided it was a good morning to brush their teeth. So they tiptoed down the hall to the bathroom in their neon-pink wedding shoes, as quietly as they could, and then down the stairs to see what—if anything—they could do for Cat.

Like moths flitting toward a lamp, the two cousins wove their way through the dark dining room toward the light peeking out from under the kitchen door. But just as they pushed the heavy door open, Willow and Delia stopped cold.

Nothing could have prepared them for what they saw.

Instead of a finished wedding cake four tiers high, they met a cake disaster. Yellow crumbs trailed across the island countertop and onto the floor. White icing was smeared on the cabinet and counter, covering part of the first tier of the cake and a good part of the kitchen. And the cake itself looked more

like a crushed wheel, flattened by something big and heavy like a bowling ball.

Cat was nowhere to be seen.

The cousins stood there frozen, hands covering their mouths. The only sound was the lingering *whoosh* from the swinging door.

"You don't think Bernice . . . ?" began Delia.

"Cat did have bacon in here last night," Willow whispered, her voice tinged with dread.

"But this seems different," Delia said, stepping closer toward the smashed cake. "Something is up, Willow. And it's not good."

"But what?"

Before Delia could answer, a frantic howl rang out from the yard. Willow reached for Delia's arm. That howl belonged to Bernice. And it could mean only one thing—Sweet William was in trouble.

Willow and Delia took off through the screen door and down the porch into the yard. Sunrise was still more than an hour away, and the grass looked a shimmery dark blue. There were boxy patches of yellow on the lawn where Cat's kitchen lights were shining through the windows.

"The garden," Delia pointed, taking a few steps in that direction. "He said he wanted an early-morning adventure. I bet he headed that way."

Willow and Delia started toward the vegetable garden, when a high-pitched peeping stopped them.

"Gossie is with them," Willow said, turning her head to listen. The sound was coming from the opposite direction. "I think they must be next door, in Cat's yard."

"Wait one second," Delia said, lifting the flouncy skirt of her flower-girl dress and racing back toward the kitchen. She was down the porch steps again in moments, yellow flashlight in hand.

The girls took off down the fence line toward the wooden gate. Delia pointed the beam of light far ahead on the path, and their ballet flats beat a steady rhythm as they cut through the dewy grass.

Another whimpering howl. Willow knew they

were getting closer.

"Do you think he's near the blueberry bushes?" Willow asked, her throat tightening at the thought of her little brother so close to the jagged bluff. What if he slipped down the side? It was a long fall to the beach below.

Gossie's peeps pierced the night, and the girls turned toward the old house.

"This way," Delia said. "It's coming from the back porch."

She raised the flashlight's beam toward the Sutherland place, and the girls stumbled their way across the yard. Bernice's bark was mournful, and they saw her pacing back and forth. Gossie's small wings flapped beside her.

But where was Sweet William?

"Would he have gone into the house without Bernice?" Delia asked, the porch steps creaking beneath her. She was shining the flashlight through the dusty black windows to peer inside.

"Sweet William doesn't go anywhere without

Bernice," Willow said. "Unless someone drags him away."

Willow's pulse was pounding in her ears, and her hands were shaking. She didn't care whether she was in trouble over the goose or the frogs or any of it. If only she could find Sweet William—that was all that mattered.

"We've got to go in there," Delia said, shining her light on the doorknob.

"I know we do," Willow agreed, clutching her cousin's hand in her own. "I just don't know what we're going to find."

The moment Willow turned the knob, Bernice pushed past them. Her nails made a clicking sound on the hardwood floor as she barreled through the rooms. Delia called after Bernice, but it was no use.

"Willow," she whispered, "get ready to do your karate thing on whatever we find in here."

"The only thing I've ever hurt doing karate"— Willow gulped—"is a wooden board!"

The paintings that lined the room seemed to be

watching as the girls crept through the unlit house, hands clinging to each other, Gossie waddling at their heels. Where were the light switches?

Murmurs from another room made them both stop.

"He's down that hall," Delia said in a hushed voice, and Willow could feel her cousin's arms tremble.

"Let's go quietly," Willow whispered. "We don't know who else is here."

Gossie was unfazed by the situation and confidently waddled ahead of them, webbed feet disappearing around the corner. Just as the girls reached the turn, their flashlight caught a white figure moving in the darkness a few feet away.

"Ghost!" Delia shrieked, dropping the flashlight and turning to run.

Willow called Sweet William's name, trying to keep her voice steady despite wanting to scream like Delia. She wasn't sure which was more unnerving— the darkness ahead of them, or knowing that always-calm, always-reasonable Delia was really and truly scared.

"Why are you guys being so loud?" came a voice.

Then Sweet William stepped into the flashlight's beam, carrying Gossie in his arms. Bernice appeared behind him, tongue hanging from her mouth and tail wagging proudly.

"Sweet William," Willow sighed, rushing forward to pull him away from the ghostlike thing behind him, "what is going on? Are you hurt?"

"I'm not the one you need to worry about," he replied. And throwing his thumb over his shoulder toward the ghost, he added, "I think she could use a little help."

Willow and Delia stared over at the ghost. Willow's throat went dry. Delia's grip tightened.

"Well, aren't you two a sight for sore eyes."

It was Cat!

Delia quickly picked up the flashlight, pointing the beam at the staircase. The ghostly figure did resemble Cat, but something wasn't right. It wasn't her hair, though it was a little messier than usual. What looked strange was her face, so pale against the dark wood behind her. White goop was smeared on her cheek. And she seemed to be wedged into the staircase rather than sitting on a step.

"Cat, wh-what's the matter?" Delia stammered. "Are you hurt?"

"I've certainly been better," she said. "Looks like I've been claimed by a creaker, and at the worst possible time."

Sweet William explained for Cat: how she'd climbed on the creaky staircase and a step had broken beneath her. And how she was stuck and couldn't pull herself out. And how he'd been on his morning adventure with Bernice and Gossie when he'd heard her calling for help.

"I think I banged up my knee pretty bad," Cat

added. "It's throbbing something awful."

Willow and Delia went to Cat's side and gently tried to pull her from the staircase. She clearly was stuck, her right leg wedged into the broken step up to her thigh. What wasn't clear, however, was why Cat smelled so sweet.

"I'm half covered in frosting," she explained, wiping a smudge of goo off her cheek and letting Bernice lick her finger clean. "Y'all know I am allergic to those flowers. Well, I must have taken too much allergy medicine, because I fell asleep right onto Rosie's wedding cake, like it was a pillow. Woke up frosted and, as you girls said, looking like a ghost."

After a few more tries, the girls finally got Cat's leg loose from the creaky stairs. They helped her hobble down a few steps to sit at the bottom. Cat let out a deep sigh and adjusted her injured knee.

"Came over here to clean myself up," she continued, "but this darn staircase got me first. I hollered for ages before Sweet William found me. He was nice enough to leave his partners outside on the porch.

You know how a Cat feels about a dog."

Especially a dog with bacon issues.

Willow was relieved that Bernice wasn't behind this latest kitchen crisis. But just thinking about Bernice eating Cat's beautiful dishes for Aunt Rosie's shower made her cringe. She began apologizing for the messes they'd made this week, and for all the trouble caused by Sweet William, Gossie, and Bernice.

"Don't say sorry for us," Sweet William huffed. "If it wasn't for Bernice hearing Cat's yells for help, we never would have found her."

Cat looked a little dumbfounded. "Imagine that." She smiled, the buttercream crackling just a little on her cheek. "I guess that makes your dog a hero."

"She sure is!" said Sweet William. And he added with a satisfied sigh, "It just goes to show that you don't have to be a grown-up to be a good person."

"But Sweet William," Delia corrected, "Bernice is a do—"

Then she caught herself. Now was not the time for setting Sweet William straight.

Chapter 19
off to the hospital

Mr. Henry rushed into the house a few minutes later, calling for Cat and switching on the lights.

"Are you awake, Ms. Catherine?" he called. "I regret to inform you that raccoons seem to have broken into the kitchen and devoured the cake you were baking. . . ."

When he reached the hallway and found them all together, Mr. Henry took his hat off in surprise. Then he put it right back on, listening as four voices began explaining at the same time. The stories were punctuated by high-pitched peeps and the occasional woof. He heard all about creakers, ghosts, and early-morning adventures before he was finally able to examine Cat's knee, which was already pretty swollen. He insisted she see a doctor right away.

"I owe it to Rosie to finish that wedding cake," Cat began. But her leg gave out as she tried to take a step.

Mr. Henry told her the wedding would go on without her, and she needed to take care of her health before taking care of a reception. But Cat kept trying to push her way down the hall and back over to Whispering Pines.

"If I don't get back in that kitchen, I'm fired," she said, leaning on Mr. Henry's arm and wincing with every step. "I'll never get another catering job. And they'll take this house right out from under me."

Willow let out a hiccup of worry that made Delia turn her head.

"She's right," Willow whispered. "If Cat fails today, the whole town is going to know about it! She's doomed!"

But Mr. Henry's voice was firm as he eased Cat

down the porch steps and into the yard, steering her toward the driveway where his blue truck was parked.

"Ms. Catherine, you've got to see a doctor. The love and devotion Rose Bumpus feels for Jonathan Baxter far exceeds the presence of a pastry. They will be wed, and they will live happily ever after—cake or no cake."

Cat looked longingly across the yard toward the big white house and her kitchen there. Willow wondered what pained Cat more—her knee, or the thought of her catering business going down the drain?

"Now, if I can settle you in peacefully," Mr. Henry said, supporting Cat's arm as she edged into the passenger seat of his truck, "I will alert the family to our predicament."

Delia said she and Willow would wait with Cat while he went into the house.

But then Willow gave her cousin's ribs a quick jab.

"Ouch!" hollered Delia. "What was that for?"

"Don't worry about a thing, Mr. Henry," Willow piped up, trying not to sound overly eager as she bounced on her toes. "Delia and I will handle whatever needs to be done here. You just get Cat to the hospital. Take care of your knee, Cat. Bye-bye!"

"Thank you, ladies," Mr. Henry said gratefully, walking around to the driver's side and climbing behind the wheel.

If it was possible for Cat to turn any whiter, she did just then. Leaning her head out the window, she sputtered, "Wh-what do you mean? What are you girls going to *handle*?"

But it was too late for conversation. Mr. Henry had already slipped the truck into reverse and was rolling down the gravel drive. Willow looped her arm through Delia's as they both waved good-bye. Sweet William, Bernice, and Gossie trailed after the blue pickup until it sped out onto the road and into the early August morning.

Chapter 20
knock knock.
who's there?

"S o what exactly are we doing?" asked Delia, her words coming out in whispered puffs as she ran beside Willow across the lawn.

"Are you kidding?" Willow puffed back, racing through the wet grass toward Whispering Pines. "You were a genius to get us up so early! With Cat gone, this is our big chance."

The yard was still dark when they reached the porch steps and dashed into the bright kitchen. Both girls stood blinking for a few moments, letting their eyes adjust to the light.

And to the disaster.

Mushed. Mashed. Squashed. Wrecked. Flattened.

Willow ran through all the words she could think of to describe Aunt Rosie's wedding cake.

"I'm not happy Cat is hurt, but you're right," Delia said a little breathlessly. Her eyes landed on the other three tiers sitting on the back counter, still waiting to be frosted. "We're going to make more than lemonade in here this morning, aren't we? This is the moment we've been waiting for!"

And they couldn't wait a second longer. Aunt Rosie was going to walk in any moment now and witness this disaster for herself. They had to get moving.

Thwack!

Delia and Willow jumped at the sound of the screen door.

"What are you guys doing?" Sweet William asked as he walked into the kitchen. He was rubbing his nose and looking curiously around Cat's countertops, Bernice and Gossie behind him. "Making pancakes?"

Willow put her arms on her brother's shoulders to march the sleepy trio back onto the porch. But Delia quickly dashed over and bolted the back door before they reached it.

"We could use him," she said. "He's definitely better off in here with us than out there explaining everything."

Out there. They were going to need a few things from out there before staying locked up in here the rest of the morning. One look at Sweet William in his rocket-ship pajamas told Willow all she needed to know about his situation.

After disappearing for what was a little longer than the blink of an eye, Willow returned to the kitchen toting Sweet William's navy wedding suit, along with her polka-dotted messenger bag (with her recipe notebook inside), Delia's new lip gloss (acquired yesterday when Sweet William found it in the yard), and a vase full of Aunt Rosie's favorite pink roses (swiped at the last minute from the dining-room table).

"I saw my mom upstairs and told her we were helping with breakfast," she panted, holding out the blue dress pants for Sweet William to take. "So she knows we're dressed and getting food. That's a start. But she'll come down here looking for us soon."

Just then they heard footsteps in the dining room, and they were getting closer. What would Aunt Rosie do if she found out about the cake? She would be as crushed as that bottom layer! And Cat's catering days would be over. Cat would never get another job in Saugatuck again!

Willow and Delia couldn't let anyone see the kitchen like this.

"The other door!" Delia hollered, lunging for the dead bolt on the swinging door to the dining room. She made it just in time. Only seconds later, the door began to rattle.

Aunt Rosie's voice. She wanted to see the cake! Delia and Willow tried not to panic. Delia started gnawing on one of her braids. Willow bit the knuckle of her index finger.

Knock knock.

"How are you doing in there, Ms. Catherine?" called Aunt Rosie in a sunny voice.

"Happy as a . . . ahh . . . pig in slop!" Delia said in her best impersonation of Cat. "Now y'all leave me be to . . . ahh . . . work."

"All right," Aunt Rosie said, sounding a little suspicious. "Are you feeling okay, Ms. Catherine? You sound a little sick."

"Just sniffly as a . . ." Delia began again. "Ahhhh . . ."

". . . a pig in slop!" Willow finished frantically.

Delia wasn't just biting her braids now. She was practically pulling them off her head. This was not going to be easy!

"I'm sorry you're feeling under the weather," Aunt Rosie said through the door. "But I know you'll do a tremendous job, no matter what."

No matter that the real Cat was at the hospital.

No matter that the wedding cake looked like a tortilla.

No matter that two fourth graders were running the kitchen.

With only a few hours left on the clock before the wedding march played, the cousins jumped into action. Willow pulled out eggs and flour and sugar as Delia searched Cat's countertops for the cake recipe. But the only cookbooks in the entire kitchen were tucked away on a corner shelf.

"She must have all her recipes memorized," Delia moaned. "What are we going to do about baking that bottom layer of cake?"

Willow grabbed her tattered notebook from the polka-dotted bag and waved it in the air. With the turn of a few pages, she tapped on a recipe.

"I call this Basic Bumpus Bellow Cake. Get it? I blended Bumpus and yellow to make *bellow*? It's pretty easy, and it's pretty delicious, too!"

Willow tried not to think about what Violet had said on the drive up to Saugatuck. She'd called her yellow cake dreadful. But Willow knew she could make it better this time around.

Delia ran her finger down the list of ingredients, opening up the refrigerator to check for items. "It looks simple enough. But Cat's out of buttermilk. We can't get around that!"

Willow's face broke into an enormous grin. Scooping up a few bright yellow lemons, she told Delia not to worry.

"Remember what Cat said? Lemons are the secret to the universe. We can use lemons to make sour milk. It works just like buttermilk. My dad showed me this trick."

Delia shook her head.

"No way. Never. *Uh-uh*," she said firmly. "This might be the most important thing we ever do in a kitchen our whole lives, Willow. We can't just wing it. It's not the time for your loosey-goosey way of doing things!"

Willow turned her eyes away, surprised at the sting from Delia's words. Suddenly all the kitchen disasters felt like her fault. Maybe she didn't know what she was doing after all. Maybe she really was just making a mess of things.

"Fine, Delia," she said angrily. "If you want everything perfect, you figure out what we should do."

Willow watched her cousin open the refrigerator

again and stare inside. Delia ran her hands over the shelves in the door. She poked her arm deep into the back corners, behind the orange juice and Cat's trays of finger foods.

Then she shut the refrigerator door with a heavy sigh. And when she looked over at Willow, her eyes were watery.

"It's not possible," Delia groaned, her voice cracking in frustration. "We cannot do this right without the right ingredients. It's impossible!"

"No, it's not impossible," Willow said, feeling more frustrated at Delia than she'd ever felt in her life. She couldn't remember ever fighting with her like this before. But then again, they'd never had a moment when so much was on the line. "It's just not possible for perfection, Delia."

The two cousins stared hard into each other's faces. Even Sweet William, Bernice, and Gossie seemed to be holding their breath. The only sound in the kitchen was the slow *drip*, *drip*, *drip* from the faucet.

"What's wrong with perfection?" Delia asked

testily. "If you're going to do something, why not do it right?"

"Maybe I am too loosey-goosey," Willow said, trying not to sound as angry as she was feeling. "But you never know how something will turn out until you give it a try."

As they faced off over the ingredients, Willow saw something flutter by the window at the sink. And Delia saw it too. Both girls stopped their fighting and watched.

It was a ruby-throated hummingbird, drawn to the window by the sweet nectar in the feeder that hung nearby. And suddenly that ruby was joined by another, and then another. Willow didn't want to move a muscle for fear that she'd scare them off and lose everything the hummingbirds' presence promised.

Overcome the impossible—that was what Delia had said.

"We can do this," Willow said slowly. "We've got to trust ourselves and try. It might not be perfect, like you want. But it will be the very best we can do."

Delia watched the hummingbirds for a few moments more, then turned her eyes toward Willow.

"Okay," Delia said softly. "But just in case we need more luck on our side, where's your wheat penny?"

Willow kicked off the neon-pink shoe from her

right foot and showed her cousin the lucky penny tucked inside. She had planned to give it to Aunt Rosie for the wedding, but now they seemed to need it more. Willow slid the ballet flat over toward Delia with her toes and told her to take it. Delia paused and looked at Willow for just a second or two before she kicked off her own right shoe and slid the copper coin inside.

"We'll do the sour milk your way," Delia finally agreed, using her calm-but-firm crossing-guard voice. "But everything else has to be exact."

Willow threw her arms around her cousin and squeezed, but their hug was interrupted by another knock at the door.

"*Yoo-hoo*, Ms. Catherine," sang Aunt Deenie, "we're searching for Mr. Henry. Have you seen him this morning?"

At the sound of her mom's voice, Delia looked like she might faint.

"Ahhh . . . he's off to the farmer's market," Willow tried in her best Cat voice. "I mean, he's fetching me some eggs." And she made *eggs* sound more like *ehhh-yuggs*.

Aunt Deenie did not seem pleased to learn that Mr.

Henry was gone, but she left the door nonetheless.

The cousins took deep breaths, then set the mixing bowl on the counter between them. Willow cracked the eggs, cautiously counting each and every one to make sure she got the number right. Delia measured the flour precisely and dumped it into the bowl, sending up an enormous poof of white dust that nearly coated the kitchen.

"Can I go find my clay?" said Sweet William, who had gotten himself dressed. "It's boring in here."

Boring? Willow was about to let him have it when Delia pointed to a stack of silver bags on the counter nearby. The labels read FONDANT. They were bags of thick icing, of every color—blue, pink, black, white, green, and yellow.

"Sweet William, I think we've just found something even better than your modeling clay," Delia said. Willow took one look at the fondant and knew exactly what her cousin had in mind.

"Now listen, because this is very important," Willow explained. "We need you to sit down and work your magic. Pretend this fondant is modeling clay. Only instead of rolling out the Clay Family, can you make us a Fondant Family? And can you make them look just like Aunt Rosie and Jonathan?"

Sweet William hung his navy suit jacket on the back of a chair and scrambled up to sit at the wide table and get to work. Bernice stretched out on the floor beneath him, and Gossie waddled over, pecking at cake crumbs before plopping down beside Bernice.

Knock knock.

"Excuse me, Ms. Cat," came another voice. "I am looking for Sweet William. Have you seen him?"

Now it was Willow's mom. Her voice was tight, the way she sounded when students mixed the nonfiction library books in with the fiction. Willow dropped her head onto the countertop and pretended to bang it. How much more could they take?

"Howdy there, Aggie," called Sweet William as he tried to mimic Cat's drawl.

"Sweet William, is that you?"

The three cousins froze. This was it—they were finally caught! Now everyone was going to know about Cat, and Aunt Rosie's wedding would be ruined.

"You guessed right, Aggie," blurted Delia, sounding remarkably like Cat herself. "That's your sweet boy." And she made *boy* sound like *bow-wee*. "He's looking handsome as a rascal and helping me with some last details. That all right with you?"

Willow's mom sounded relieved that Cat and

Sweet William were getting along. So she gave them her blessing.

But she wasn't done.

"And one more thing, Ms. Catherine," she said politely. "Have you seen Willow and Delia? We're ready to style their hair for the wedding. They'll both be wearing buns."

"Buns!" cried Willow with a look of disgust. And then she slapped a hand over her mouth to keep from making any more outbursts.

"What did you say?" asked her mom.

"I burned my honey buns," Delia said quickly in her Cat voice. "Got to get back to cooking. Good-bye now!"

Sweet William's Fondant Family

Ingredients:

2 cups powdered sugar

¼ cup milk

¼ cup vegetable shortening

1 teaspoon vanilla extract

Directions:

1. Make sure you have an adult's help.

2. Using an electric mixer, blend the sugar and milk. Add the vegetable shortening and vanilla. Mix together until a smooth dough forms.

3. Separate dough into thirds and put each third in its own bowl. Drop food coloring into each bowl and blend with the electric mixer. Be sure to clean your beaters each time you change bowls; otherwise you'll muddy your colors.

4. If the dough is sticky, add more powdered sugar until it becomes smoother.

5. Sculpt fondant into any shape, from animals to flowers to people. Or use wax paper and a rolling pin to flatten out the fondant and drape it over your cake. Be sure to frost the cake first.

Chapter 21
showtime!

before long, the bottom tier of Aunt Rosie's cake was baked, cooled in the freezer, and frosted white. The cousins stacked the other three layers on top of it, alternating the icing from white to pink. And now, with the last of the pink icing smoothed into place on the top layer, Delia and Willow were ready to begin the process of decorating it.

They snipped pink roses from the vase and arranged the flowers here and there on the second tier and the top one, where they matched the pink icing perfectly. But what could they put on the two white layers?

"We need something pink there, too. . . ." Willow said, circling the kitchen in search of a cake decoration and nearly tripping over the polka-dotted bag. "Something Aunt Rosie loves. But it can't be more pink roses. If only we had something special."

Delia pointed at the bag, nearly jumping off her stool. "We do have something special. Aunt Rosie's favorites!"

Willow opened the polka-dotted bag and dumped out what was left of Aunt Rosie's candies.

Delia suggested they trim the edges of the pink tiers with the white Mentos, creating a scalloped line that would look fancy. Willow thought they should position the Good & Plenty just so around the first and third tiers, laying the pieces like mosaic tiles on a white-icing wall: pink pink, white white, pink pink, white white, in a pattern all the way around.

"This cake is a little bit of both of us," Willow pronounced, stepping back to marvel at their creation. "And a whole lot of Aunt Rosie."

"Don't forget me!" Sweet William shouted from the table. "My Found-It Family is ready!"

"Fondant," Delia corrected. "And they're just perfect."

Willow and Delia dragged over two chairs to stand on, then gingerly added Sweet William's fondant creations to the very top. After they spent a few more minutes tinkering here and there with final touches (and wrestling with Bernice to keep her from licking the frosting), the sounds of the musicians practicing on the lawn let them know it was showtime.

Willow's mom and Aunt Deenie had just begun banging on the door from the dining room in search of their children when Willow unlocked the outside door to the porch. Delia quickly slipped Sweet William's arms into his jacket. Willow ran her fingers through his loopy hair, smoothing down the craziest curls.

The screen door made a *thwack* as they emerged onto the porch and down the back steps, Bernice galumphing behind them and Gossie waddling to keep up.

Willow grabbed Delia's hand as they stepped into the busy yard, and she squeezed it tight. Delia's quick squeeze back told Willow she was feeling the same way—tense and excited and eager to see what might happen next. And that was when a strange thought occurred to Willow:

This must be what Violet feels like just before her swim meets.

Chapter 22
the flour girls

good heavens! You girls look dreadful in those flower-girl dresses," Grandma said.

"That's what we've been trying to tell everyone all along!" Willow and Delia exclaimed together.

But Grandma was shaking her head and shoving a pink bouquet into each girl's hand, ushering them along. "There's no time to change! Now go!"

The yard was already filled with guests, and Reverend Roland was nodding to them from the far end of the red carpet, where he stood beside Jonathan, who was grinning his crooked grin and looking nervous. Uncle Delvan stepped in front of the girls and put his arm out for Grandma to take, escorting her down the aisle to her seat like he was a prince. Willow couldn't believe how handsome he looked in his navy suit jacket and tie.

Listening for the right beat of the wedding march, Delia and Willow took their first few steps down the aisle at exactly the same time. But something didn't seem right. The hundred guests gathered in the yard were supposed to be friends and family members. But as the two cousins passed the faces lining the aisle, not one of them was smiling back. They were frowning, as if Delia and Willow were giving off a horrible smell.

Willow looked over at her cousin for some clue as to what was going on. And she got her answer right away—Delia was a mess! With all the excitement of finishing the cake, she hadn't even noticed that Delia's cheeks were smudged with flour. Or that one of her black braids was dusted in white powder!

"Ohhh," Delia gasped, pointing back at Willow. "Your dress!"

When Willow glanced down, she saw for the first time what she looked like. Her own dress was coated in flour! Instead of that awful shade of bubble-gum pink, now her gown was a lighter shade of blush. She thought it was a tremendous improvement, and she couldn't stop the hiccup of laughter that suddenly escaped her mouth. Delia buried her face in her bouquet to keep from laughing. But it was no use, and she threw her head back and let loose, too.

"I think we look perfect," Willow murmured.

"And even if we get in trouble for this," Delia

whispered, her eyes dancing from Willow's powdered gown to her own, "it was worth it! We might have saved Aunt Rosie's wedding day."

"Or maybe even more than that," Willow whispered back.

With Aunt Rosie's wedding cake waiting in the kitchen and their hopes for Cat's catering growing by the minute, being stuck in medicine-drink pink wasn't nearly as bad as they'd imagined.

Reverend Roland raised his eyebrows as the flower girls reached the top of the aisle. And Jonathan gave them each a kiss on the forehead, quickly wiping flour from his lips once they'd passed.

The music played on, and the crowd turned back to the aisle to watch the next pair making its way up to Jonathan. For once in her life, Willow was actually thankful to have her big sister steal all the attention away. It felt much better having the crowd's eyes on Violet and Darlene rather than on her and Delia's messy flower-girl dresses.

Their sisters seemed to glide down the red carpet

like a couple of summer swans. Willow couldn't help but notice how sophisticated they looked in their rich purple gowns. She fluffed her skirt to try to get rid of some of the flour. Delia dusted at her cheek.

Willow's mom and Aunt Deenie were next as matrons of honor, a title Willow thought made them sound old and fat. They looked anything but, however, as they marched down the aisle, giggling and excited. Aunt Deenie had pinned a soft pink rose in her hair. Willow looked at her mom's, and she could swear she saw a pencil tucked in there.

Delia peeked over at her dad on the other side of Jonathan. "Does he see how beautiful my mom looks today?" she whispered.

Both their mothers were like giddy birthday girls at a slumber party—that is, until their eyes landed on Delia and Willow and all the flour they were wearing. Their faces fell at the sight of the flower girls, and Delia and Willow began to squirm under their gaze.

But just then, fierce growling erupted from the

aisle. All heads turned to the end of the red carpet to see what the commotion was about. It was Sweet William, growling and snapping his jaws at the wedding guests as he carried his little white pillow with the gold wedding rings attached. There was a wave of quiet laughter from the crowd, but Willow's mom and Aunt Deenie were not smiling.

Willow felt another rush of gratitude for her siblings, who were doing such a good job of drawing attention away from her and Delia and their powdery gowns.

Before her little brother could snarl at Reverend Roland, Jonathan put a hand on Sweet William's shoulder. "What are you doing?" he asked, grinning from ear to ear and leaning down so he could hear his soon-to-be nephew.

"I'm a ring bear," Sweet William said with a shrug. "Isn't that what you asked me to be?"

A different song began to play, and all the guests rose to their feet. There was Grandpa, smiling and proud and walking Aunt Rosie down the aisle. She

was beaming beside him in her simple, sleek white gown. Willow kept her eyes on Jonathan, who seemed to melt as he watched Aunt Rosie approach. Jonathan shook Grandpa's hand and then took Aunt Rosie's in his own. Before Willow knew it, vows were exchanged, the kiss was planted, and the rest of the wedding party was marching back down the aisle.

But Willow and Delia stood still, leaning close together and hiding behind their bouquets. What was Aunt Rosie going to say about the cake? What were their moms going to say about their dresses? And what was everyone going to say about the angry Mother Goose pacing back and forth behind the photographer?

Willow eyed the bluff overlooking the water. Should they make a break for it? Scramble down the side and hope they found a smooth path to the beach?

Willow's mom began making her way toward them from one side of the yard, shoveling past guests like a snowplow through a Chicago winter. Aunt Deenie was storming up the other side, pointing at them with her bouquet of roses. Willow was just turning her body to run for it when a yell went up across the yard.

"It's Cat!" Violet and Darlene were hollering, waving their moms over to the enormous white reception tent with big scoops of their arms. "And it doesn't look good!"

A gasp erupted from the wedding guests as everyone gathered around Cat and Mr. Henry.

"What now?" huffed Willow's mom. And she and Aunt Deenie wove their way back through the rows of white folding chairs, leaving Willow and Delia in the floury dust.

Cat was leaning on Mr. Henry's arm, looking pale and exhausted. Her hair was loose and billowing in the wind, and on her leg was a long white brace.

"I'm not dead, y'all . . ." Willow heard her say in a choked voice. And then, when Cat caught sight of Aunt Rosie and Jonathan, she added, "Yet. I'm afraid I ruined your wedding day, Rosie."

That was just the distraction Delia and Willow

needed to escape. They sprinted down the red carpet and over to the edge of the crowd, tugging Darlene and Violet by the arms.

"Listen, Violet," Willow began. "We need you guys. Cat couldn't finish Aunt Rosie's wedding cake. So we . . ."

"So we did," Delia said, squaring her shoulders and looking hard at Darlene. She was braced for a fight.

"You did what?" Darlene exclaimed. "Delia, you two are just a couple of little kids! There's no way—"

Willow interrupted, turning from the Dees sisters to her own. She had to make Violet understand how important this moment was—not just for herself and for Delia, but for Aunt Rosie and Cat, too.

"Violet, please," she began, searching her sister's eyes. "For once, I might have finally done something right."

To Willow's great relief, Violet nodded.

"I get it," Violet said. "I really do."

Willow and Delia took off around the back of the

house, Violet falling in right behind them, Darlene joining beside her. They raced up the porch steps and into the kitchen.

"I don't believe it," was all either of their big sisters could say as they circled the cake. "How could you guys have possibly done this?"

"Ready? Lift on the count of three," Delia called. "One, two . . ."

"Wait!"

Willow stepped back from the center island with a start. Now, instead of Delia being the worrier, it was Willow's turn. Suddenly she was the one who wanted to be precise. What if they made a mistake lifting the cake? What if it toppled over when they tried to move it to the yard? What if they made an even bigger disaster of things?

"Come on, Willow," Violet said with an encouraging smile. "This thing is amazing. I want everyone to see what my little sister did."

Willow rattled her head back and forth as if she had water in her ears. A compliment? From Violet?

She looked over at Delia, who stuck out her foot and jiggled the shoe that held the wheat penny. Willow and Delia couldn't help but laugh. So far, their luck hadn't run out.

"Okay," Willow said, sucking in a big breath. "One. Two. Three!"

As delicately as possible, the foursome picked up the board that held the wedding cake. They carried it back through the screen door, gingerly down the porch steps, and around the far side of the yard to the white reception tent flapping in the breeze.

With slow, coordinated movements, they placed it on the cake table, front and center, beside the special knife and pink plates. No one else seemed to notice them, since Cat was holding court in the yard, telling her story of honeysuckle and too much allergy medicine. Aunt Rosie and Jonathan were patting her shoulders with concern.

"Don't look at me," Cat said in embarrassment. "I fell out of the ugly tree and hit every branch on the way down."

Just then, the crowd around Cat parted. Bernice ran through, barking and wagging with delight. Sweet William skipped past next, munching a cucumber instead of waving it this time. And last came Gossie, waddling excitedly behind them.

"At this point, those critters can take all the vegetables they want," Cat said sadly. "It's over for me."

"Perhaps not," said Mr. Henry, clearing his throat. "Perhaps it's time you know the truth."

Cat stood there dumbfounded, or at least as dumbfounded as anyone who had fallen asleep on a wedding cake, gotten stuck in a broken staircase, and just hobbled home from the hospital possibly could.

"Henry Rickles," she said. "What . . . ?"

"It is I," he began, removing his sun hat, then putting it right back on again. "I have been taking your tomatoes, collecting your cucumbers. And I confess that it is I who has been stealing your sauce."

When Cat asked him what for, Mr. Henry turned three different shades of pink. "For the past few weeks, I've been selling them at the farmers market. I thought if more people got a taste of Catherine Sutherland's remarkable way with food," he said, his voice softening, "well, they might fall in love, too."

The crowd gathered around them let out *oooooh*s and *aaaaah*s. And even Aunt Rosie and Jonathan looked swept up by all the extra romance in the air.

"His cheeks are as pink as that wedding cake," chuckled one of the guests. And that sent all eyes turning back to the big white tent where Willow and Delia were standing. Violet, Darlene, and Sweet William were lined up beside them, Bernice wagging proudly nearby, and Gossie, too.

Willow's heart was pounding in her ears, and Delia was gnawing on one of her braids—that is until Darlene noticed and yanked it out of her mouth. Then, just as Aunt Rosie and Jonathan approached, the cousins silently stepped apart to reveal the wedding cake.

There it was. Four tiers, just as Aunt Rosie had wanted, only all the more special because they featured a few of her favorite things. Her eyes went to the bottom layer first, taking in the smooth white frosting and the pink-and-white candy mosaic. Aunt Rosie's hand fluttered to her cheek. She looked at the second tier, where the perfectly round Mentos circled the edge of the neat pink frosting.

Aunt Rosie reached out and touched the pale pink roses. She dabbed at her eyes. Jonathan wrapped his arm around her shoulder and gave it an affectionate squeeze as their gaze climbed up to the third tier and the Good & Plenty pattern there.

But the best part was on top. When Aunt Rosie saw it, she began to cry. Sweet William had worked his magic, creating the perfect likeness of Aunt Rosie in her white wedding dress and Jonathan—Uncle Jonathan—in his dark blue suit.

Even their smiles were true to life. Uncle Jonathan's was just a little lopsided.

"I don't know how you did it," said Aunt Rosie, turning to face Delia and Willow, her expression a bit stunned. "But you girls just made my day even more special. I think I might have underestimated the two of you."

Just then Cat hobbled through the crowd, finally catching sight of the wedding cake.

"I don't believe it," she gasped. "This is marvelous!"

Cat scanned the faces surrounding the cake until

she found Delia and Willow. Rushing to their sides (with a lot of help from Mr. Henry), she took their hands in hers.

"I can't thank you girls enough," she said, tears making their way from the corners of her eyes and down her cheeks, one still faintly smudged with frosting. "Y'all saved my hide. And I'll never, ever forget it."

Cat threw her arms around both Delia and Willow, and neither cousin seemed to care about getting smudged by the buttercream that was still clumped in Cat's hair. What was a little frosting when they were already covered in flour?

"How in the world did you have time to finish this?" she asked, draping an arm around each girl's shoulders.

"We locked ourselves in the kitchen and didn't come out until it was perfect." Willow shrugged, feeling a little amazed by what they'd pulled off.

"Plus we sort of winged it," said Delia, poking Willow in the side.

Willow's dad stepped over, wearing a serious

expression that made Willow a little nervous. Was she going to get in trouble after all?

"I'm so sorry, Dad," she began, trying to sneak in a quick explanation. "Sweet William has a pet gosling. I didn't mean to let him—"

"And there's no way it will imprint back on its mother," Delia added. "Gossie has to live with humans."

He patted Delia on the shoulder and stared at her for a moment, obviously impressed with her knowledge of goose trivia. Then he turned to Willow and tilted her chin up to face him, looking her square in the eye.

"I'm not worried about pets right now," he said with a smile. "Willow, you girls really outdid yourselves today. A four-star performance."

Willow threw her arms around her dad's shoulders and felt her feet lift off the ground. She wanted to tell him it was all because of him, but the words got stuck in her throat.

"Mom has her hankie working overtime," he whispered. "You've made us both so proud."

Chapter 23

a few more summer surprises

You look so good, Henry Rickles, I want to sop you up with a biscuit!"

Delia and Willow were on their way down to the beach for one last boogie-boarding session when they passed the screen door to the kitchen, where Mr. Henry and Cat were talking. Grandma and Grandpa had already started down the bluff staircase with Sweet William and Bernice. Gossie waddled along with them, now an honorary member of the family after last night's wedding reception and endless ukulele sing-alongs.

"Should we go in and talk to Mr. Henry now?" Delia asked.

"I don't know," Willow said, rubbing sunblock across her nose. "It has to happen soon, but can we talk in front of Cat?"

The girls didn't have time to decide, because Cat caught sight of them and opened the screen door to invite them in.

"Here are my girls." She smiled warmly. "I should never have doubted what you could do in the kitchen. You were born to bake, the both of y'all."

Beaming with pride, Willow was too happy to speak. So Delia did the talking, forgetting her calm crossing-guard voice in all the excitement about the wedding. Once the fussing had finally finished, Delia signaled Mr. Henry that they needed to talk.

Privately.

"What about your jars of Cat's vegetable sauce?" she began a little breathlessly. "Could you sell them at the café, too?"

Delia's hopes had become wrapped up in the

gallery-café idea, and she'd already told Willow she couldn't bear to pack her suitcase and head back to Detroit in a few hours without someone sitting down and talking to her dad and mom about it.

"I promise to speak to them," Mr. Henry said earnestly, walking them down the porch and out of earshot from Cat. "Your ideas are wonderful, girls, and they show how much you truly care—about your father, Delia, about Ms. Catherine, and about the specialness of Whispering Pines. But you can't get your hopes up. Sometimes change is hard, and I'm sorry to say it gets harder as we get older."

Mr. Henry suggested they go down to the beach and enjoy their last hurrah in the water. He promised to fill them in the minute they came back up.

"There you are," called Uncle Delvan when Willow and Delia stepped back into the yard a while later. "Rosie and Jonathan are leaving for their honeymoon soon. Would you mind running upstairs and getting the present we hid under your bed, Delia?"

Delia and Willow kicked off their flip-flops and took off into the house before Grandma, Grandpa, and the others had even finished climbing the staircase from the beach. They raced back with the present, and it was only then, as they set it down on the porch where Aunt Rosie and Uncle Jonathan were sitting, that they noticed the paper was torn and the frame's corner chipped.

"Uncle Delvan," Willow said as the rest of the family gathered around, "I think we broke it, probably when we had our fort war. I'm so sorry."

"It's my fault," Delia said, her eyes suddenly wet. "It's because of me that it's broken—that nothing is right."

Uncle Delvan stepped over to Delia and scooped her up in his arms like she was a little girl. Delia even buried her head in his neck the way Sweet William did when he fell off his scooter and needed comforting. Uncle Delvan rubbed her back for a minute or two as Aunt Deenie kissed her hands, then he set her feet back on the ground.

"Not to worry, girls," Uncle Delvan said. "Maybe we can fix it next door."

Next door?

Delia looked from her dad's face to Willow's. She stepped back up onto the porch to stand beside her cousin. Willow grabbed Delia's hand and held it tight. Suddenly Whispering Pines felt charged with something, like a strange electricity was in the air.

Grandpa and Grandma, her sun hat ringed with pink roses from the wedding, climbed the porch steps and took their usual seats in the white wicker chairs. Violet and Darlene, who were eating grape Popsicles, perched themselves on the edge of the small table between their grandparents. Willow's mom and dad sat on the porch steps, and Aunt Deenie stood on the grass beside Uncle Delvan. Mr. Henry and Cat, her stiff leg brace sticking out to the side, were seated in porch chairs next to Jonathan and Rosie.

"We were talking with Mr. Henry this morning," Uncle Delvan began slowly, "and we were thinking maybe we won't come to Whispering

Pines each August anymore."

Delia made a sound that Willow feared was a sob trying to get out. She squeezed Delia's hands reassuringly. Don't cry, Delia, that squeeze said, even though Willow felt close to tears herself.

How could they stop coming to Whispering Pines? After all these years, the place was in their blood.

What was summer without chasing fireflies and picking blueberries?

What would happen to the hummingbirds without Willow and Delia keeping watch?

Willow tried to catch Mr. Henry's eye. His talk with their parents must have gone terribly.

"What if," Uncle Delvan continued slowly, "we were here all the time?" And he wrapped his arm around Aunt Deenie and kissed her cheek. "Girls, how would you like to leave Detroit and make a fresh start? What if we try living at the Sutherland place next door?"

Delia flew down the porch stairs without her feet seeming to touch a single step. Darlene was down in a flash, too, hugging their mom and dad.

Willow was so surprised and relieved and happy that she threw her arms around the nearest person she could find. It happened to be Violet, who at first gave Willow a stunned look, but then found herself just as excited as her little sister.

"This all started with Delia and Willow," Aunt Deenie began, one arm wrapped around Uncle Delvan's waist and the other around Darlene. But her eyes were fixed on Delia.

"They had a pretty good idea. They thought Cat should take the old house next door and try to restore the place to what it once was—an art gallery. They thought Daddy could get back to his first love, making art."

Uncle Delvan said something about Aunt Deenie being his first love, which made Delia start crying for real now. So Willow scooted down the porch steps to her side.

"Uncle Delvan figured if he is going to paint again, why not do it right here in Saugatuck?" Willow's mom explained. "Aunt Deenie thinks she can get hired with the hospital. And as for us, well, that means we could come back any time Aunt Deenie and Uncle Delvan will have us. Not just for one week in August."

Willow turned to Delia, and they began to shriek and jump up and down like they'd won a bake-off. Bernice and Gossie got swept up in the commotion and began barking and wagging and peeping beside them. Sweet William flapped his arms as well, then hopped over to his dad for a piggyback ride. Willow and Delia fell to the ground laughing like complete lunatics as their sisters clucked their disapproval.

"And that's why you will never be junior brides-maids," Violet said.

Or maybe it was Darlene. Willow didn't care who said it. She just knew it sounded hilarious. She and Delia dissolved into such hysterics that they had tears pouring down their faces and their stomachs began to ache.

"Now what do you make of this, dear?" they heard Grandma saying to Grandpa. "All along, I suspected

they were trying to get out of being flower girls. But then they go and save Rosie's wedding reception. And now this! Look who's growing up."

Willow saw them both gazing down at her and Delia sprawled on the lawn.

"I'd say *starting* to grow up might be more like it," Grandpa said, grinning. "They're blossoming."

Once they'd gotten to their feet, Willow remembered something. Where was Mr. Henry? There were questions that needed answering. They ran back up the porch steps to where he and Cat were seated. The rest of the family pressed in to hear.

"Mr. Henry," began Delia breathlessly, "what about opening the café?"

"Ms. Catherine and the others loved the idea," he answered calmly.

"Mr. Henry," Willow said, "what about fixing up the house? How will—"

"Delvan and Deenie will do what they can, your grandparents will do the gardening and landscape the grounds, and contractors will do the rest," he replied, pausing for the next question he seemed to know was coming.

Delia got there first.

"Mr. Henry," she asked, pausing this time, "where exactly will Cat live when my family moves into the yellow house—"

And Willow spotted the answer right there, on the third finger of Cat's left hand. It was a ring with a beautiful red stone surrounded by glittering diamonds.

"I'll be living over here from now on," said Cat, batting her eyelashes at Mr. Henry, who turned a darker shade of pink. "He dropped onto one knee in the kitchen and gave me a ruby ring, to match my beloved rubies."

"I prefer to think of that jewel as my tribute to your tomatoes," said Mr. Henry, smiling and holding her hand in his. "But I think either interpretation is appropriate."

Willow and Delia erupted into cheers and squeals of joy that rivaled fireworks at the Fourth of July, jumping up and down and hugging and laughing for the second time that morning. With Delia's family living here year-round, it was like their vacation would never end. And with Cat running her own café, well, Willow could only imagine what it would be like to help out. Maybe she really could be a sous-chef after all.

A hummingbird flitted by just then, making its way from a cluster of flowers up to a feeder at the end of the porch. Cat saw it and smiled. "I think y'all will make wonderful junior bridesmaids some day."

Delia and Willow exchanged hopeful looks.

"Will you have a big wedding?" Willow wondered with a particularly springy bounce.

"And will you need someone to make the food?" Delia grinned beside her.

"I must say," chuckled Mr. Henry with a shake of his head, "of everyone who comes back to Whispering Pines each summer, you two girls certainly take the cake."

"You can say that again," laughed Willow, throwing an arm around Delia's shoulder. "And we sure bake a mean one, too."

Willow & Delia's Basic Bumpus Bellow Cake Cupcakes

Ingredients:

3 cups flour

1 tablespoon baking powder

1½ cups sugar

1 teaspoon salt

1 cup (2 sticks) butter,
softened but not melted

3 eggs

1 tablespoon vanilla

1 cup buttermilk or sour
milk*

* To make sour milk, pour 1 tablespoon lemon juice in a
measuring cup, then add enough milk to equal 1 cup liquid.
Set aside until ready to use.

Directions:

1. Make sure you have an adult's help.

2. Heat oven to 350 degrees. Line two 12-cup muffin tins with cupcake wrappers.

3. In a mixing bowl, add together the flour, baking powder, sugar, and salt.

4. Using an electric mixer, beat in the softened butter, eggs, and vanilla.

5. Pour in the buttermilk or sour milk.

6. Once everything is blended together, spoon the batter into the lined muffin tins.

7. Bake for about 18 to 20 minutes or until a toothpick inserted into the center of a cupcake comes out clean.

8. Set on a wire rack to cool completely, about 30 minutes.

Makes 24 cupcakes.

Aunt Rosie's Pink and White Frosting

Ingredients:

1 cup (2 sticks) butter, softened but not melted

6 to **8** cups powdered sugar

½ cup milk

2 teaspoons vanilla

Red food coloring

Directions:

1. Make sure you have an adult's help.

2. Using an electric mixer, put the softened butter in a large bowl and add 4 cups powdered sugar. Beat together, adding the milk and vanilla. Mix until smooth and creamy.

3. Gradually add the remaining sugar, 1 cup at a time. Beat for 1 to 2 minutes, until the icing is creamy and perfect for spreading. (You might not need all of the sugar.)

4. Separate out half the icing into a new bowl. This is your white frosting.

5. For the pink, use the remaining icing still in the mixing bowl. Add a few drops of red food coloring. Mix the icing thoroughly to get the exact color of pink that Aunt Rosie loves. (Hint: Think pink roses!)

6. Spread cupcakes with either the pink or the white frosting. Cover the top with pink and white candies such as Good & Plenty to create a pink-and-white mosaic. Crown with a Mentos, which can look like a white cherry on top. Or add your own fondant creations.

7. Arrange your cupcakes on a cake plate or cupcake tree. And get ready to work at the next wedding or party that you're invited to attend!